BEHIND THE MIRAGE

BEHIND THE MIRAGE

A NOVEL

KATHARINE ANN MELTON

FIRELIGHT
PRESS

FIRELIGHT
PRESS

PUBLISHED BY FIRELIGHT PRESS
FAIRFAX, VA

Edited by Lauren Taylor Shute Editorial
Cover design by Hampton Lamoureux

Library of Congress Number in progress.
Paperback: 978-1-7355765-1-0
Ebook: 978-1-7355765-0-3
KDP: 978-1-7355765-2-7

Printed in the United States of America

First edition

For my family and friends.
When the desire to quit was overwhelming,
you were there to remind me to never give up,
no matter the outcome.

One year earlier...

*A*valon is beautiful, a secret place that most beings in the human world don't realize exists—perhaps they have only imagined it as a myth. It lies just beyond the Pindus and Rodopi mountains in Greece. If you stare long enough between the mountains, past the point when everyone looks away and forgets the mirage that never quite resolves, your eyes will focus on the mythical island that is my home. Not many venture that far—it's gone just when you glance at it. It's a place where immortal creatures live an eternal life, where the enforcers of the Gods keep the peace between the human world and the world of the Gods. A white stone castle sits high above a cliff looking out to the ocean. Trees hued the brightest of neon to the darkest of emerald flourish as if they've always been full of life and energy. Exotic flowers with colors that have never reached the world of man sparkle opalescent pink and shimmer like purple-orange fire with a touch of gold. The ocean is so clear you can see to the bottom, and sometimes farther, into the depths of the abyss. It's a very peaceful place.

Maybe too peaceful. Every moment, I dream of leaving this place because part of me has always felt like I don't belong. Turns out there's a reason for that, but I'm jumping ahead.

I sit on the edge of a rock, my feet lightly splashing in the cool water. The ocean expands past my line of vision, touching nothing but the edge of the Earth, wherever that is. A light mist rolls in, engulfing the moss-covered rocks like a tattered blanket. I've been sitting here most of the day, daydreaming once again, and night has fallen too quickly. The stars shine brightly, asking me to come play with them as they light my way to the world beyond this one; the world I want to explore more than anything.

To visit that outside place and experience its glory would wake a part of me that has been asleep since the death of my parents. Oberon, the Fae king, took me under his wing and raised me as his own. He's always watched over me and taught me, giving me ultimate power as one of his most experienced assassins. That's why his recent proposal had taken me by surprise.

"Lex."

Oberon's voice floated through the air, sweet yet sinful, pulling me from my thoughts. I turned and gazed up at the magnificent power that stared down at me. My feelings for Oberon have always been paternal. Lately, he has been eager for me to make a decision about our future together. I've told him I'm flattered, but I don't yearn to marry him. He wasn't taking me seriously.

I tried to stand, being careful to avoid falling into the sea as he offered a hand to help me. I sensed his admiration, his longing for me. His beautiful eyes stared down at me.

"Yes, my king?"

He smiled faintly. "Your beautiful voice sends chills down my body."

I internally rolled my eyes. Here we go again.

"My deepest desire is for you to see me not only as your protector, but also as your lover."

"Oberon..." I began.

He resumed his speech, cutting me off. "There is a threat to the human world that could cross onto our shores if it is not handled immediately." He paused, and I looked at him in anticipation. "I want you to descend upon the world of man, eradicate this threat, and return to me and accept the throne I've offered you. I won't wait any longer, Lex."

I was without words. It didn't matter that I'd turned down his proposal—this was a command. I ducked his embrace and asked about his first order. "Why send me to the human world?"

He sighed greatly. "You are my best assassin and I know you will triumph where others would fail. And your fascination with the human world lights a fire in your eyes that I hardly ever see." He paused. "One that I have not seen for a very long time."

That was true. I had wanted to travel for as long as I could remember. The human world was a guilty pleasure for me. I would watch the humans from Oberon's throne room. I would look in the reflecting pool that lay at the altar and watch humans spend time in cafés and small shops—laughing, as though life was perfect. I brought myself back to the current conversation. Did he just say something about a threat? "What do you mean by 'a threat'? What are you talking about?"

"The ocean can feel it. It can anticipate the sudden change in the balance of man and our home. We may not stay hidden for much longer. This fear has haunted my dreams for nearly a thousand years." He touches my cheek. "Zeus, the King of the Gods, has threatened to, as he says, 'take back the world which he birthed.' The time has come to show the humans I rule their lives and can crush them without a moment's thought.'"

"What does this have to do with us?" I asked.

His hand glided away from my cheek and he stroked my arm before walking past me. His touch made me uncomfortable, a little awkward. He stood at the edge of the rocks, looking out toward the sea. I stared at his back, contemplating that discomforting caress. I worried for him, as a child would worry for a parent who was struggling with the idea that their family was in jeopardy. I wasn't sure he'd give up his pursuit of me.

"A thousand years ago, during a great battle, we allied with the humans and the Old Ones: the demons. We battled till the streets ran with blood. All sides—the Fae, the humans, and the demons —suffered many losses. Zeus's own children rose against him because he forced them to fight. He lost his love for the humans, said they were a deceiving and vile race. He wanted them eradicated from this world. I decided the best course of action was to cast him out. He was losing his grip and the humans were losing their faith in him."

"I know all of this; I've heard the stories. Zeus found out you planned to overthrow him, so he went into hiding in Tartarus. His imperial guards joined our side and went after him, but he disappeared."

"You do not know the whole story, Lex. Zeus left Tartarus and escaped to the human world. Rumor spread that during his escape, your parents were caught in the middle."

My insides did a somersault. "What do you mean?" I asked cautiously. I wanted to jump out of my skin as I waited for him to answer my question. A terrible thought entered my mind. I asked a question I wasn't sure I wanted answered. "Did he murder my parents?"

Oberon turned. Grief and shame showed all over his delicate face. For a moment, I saw a slight sparkle in his eyes—then it was gone. He struggled to form the words, to find a way to tell me what I already knew, to offer some soft words to ease my pain. Something tugged at my senses; he was different in that moment, satisfied. It was unsettling.

"Yes," he said with a touch of haste.

I tried to breathe. Vulnerability made you weak. Feelings always got in the way of duty, and I never wanted mine to be used against me. I was angry; I wanted Zeus's head.

Crickets chirped somewhere in the night. The moon's reflection sparkled brightly on the ocean.

"What do you need from me?" I asked.

"I want you to find Zeus and take him out before he can return to Mount Olympus and reclaim the throne. I'm afraid if he isn't stopped, he will destroy our home and every being that resides here. There are whispers that the Old Ones have returned."

"Do you know where Zeus might be? And why now? Why is this so urgent?"

I had so many questions. This had all happened a thousand years ago. If Zeus escaped Tartarus, wouldn't he have already retaken the throne and exacted his revenge?

A smile bloomed on Oberon's face. He read me so easily; my eyes give everything away.

"Zeus made it clear how much he despised the humans. The most logical place for him to be is in their world. Lucian has contacts in Greece who have sighted him in Plaka, a neighborhood in Athens. I don't know why Zeus waited this long, but it doesn't matter. Don't forget, Lex, he is responsible for the death of your parents."

How could I forget—I'd been waiting years for the truth. "Who is Lucian's contact?"

"His name is Akesios."

"I'll go," I said.

Oberon smiled down at me. "Please be careful. The sooner you resolve this the better it will be for all of us. I sense that there are others looking for Zeus as well. Be wary of who you trust, Lex."

I gave him a reassuring look. I would not let Oberon down—too much was at stake and this assignment was an honor. Another upside to all this, besides killing Zeus, would be time away from Oberon; a pause to contemplate my life and what I wanted out of it. To say I was excited was an understatement.

I hadn't been outside the walls of Avalon in ages. I remember when I was younger, my mother caught me in Oberon's throne room staring into the reflecting pool. She told me I spent too much time daydreaming about places I would never go. I was eager to walk through those worlds. My whole life I had been looked at as the fragile one; the protected one. I was forbidden from exploring Avalon like the other kids. I wasn't allowed to dive off Lanos Mountain, a thirty-foot cliff that peered over the Mediterranean Sea. With effort, I convinced Oberon to allow me to train with the Sikarios, his highly skilled assassins.

After my conversation with Oberon, my mind churned. I was so consumed with my thoughts as I walked, that I didn't see Lucian until I literally ran into him. He grabbed my shoulders to steady me. I looked into his eyes and a wave of nausea hit. I jerked out of his grasp. Lucian had been my mentor. He was the most respected mentor among the Fae, but he had begun enjoying his duty too much.

"If you don't keep an eye on where you're going, you might just end up somewhere you don't wanna be," Lucian said.

His smile used to calm me. Now it just gives me the creeps. "Stay away from me, Lucian."

"Such fire. That's why you were my best student—so much power."

"I'm leaving," I said.

"You better watch yourself, Lex. You might be Oberon's pet, but you're not infallible," Lucian called after me.

MY APARTMENT WASN'T FAR, and I'd left the lights on—something I often do. It gives me a sense that I'm coming home to something. Home...soon I'll be leaving it behind. Though it hasn't felt like home for a long time.

In Avalon, our homes and apartments are not much different

from those in the human world. My apartment didn't have much: a small dinette set in the corner, a flat-screen TV on top of the mantel, a silver and gray couch, and a light-blue armchair. I didn't have pictures on the wall; I didn't have books or anything else that made a place a home. Guess I always knew my life would be heading in a different direction—I was just waiting for the right time. I opened the refrigerator and grabbed the last bottle of wine, deciding to forgo a glass and drink straight from the bottle. I kicked off my boots and fell into the plush armchair. I'd just started on the bottle when there was a knock at my door. *Ugh.* Bottle in hand, I walked over to the door and opened it. Marius, my best friend, stood on the other side.

"I guess the rumors are true then?" he said jokingly.

Marius and I met during training. We'd been paired off and I remember him saying he got the short end of the stick because I was smaller than the other girls. He was trying to be the big man on campus by showing off and making a fool out of me. Unfortunately for him, it only resulted in my fist to his face and him on his back. We'd been best friends ever since.

"What rumors?"

"That you're a loser," he smiled, and I stepped aside, letting him in. He strolled straight to the fridge, noticed I had no beer, and snatched the wine bottle out of my hand.

"Hey!" I squealed.

"Go shopping," he laughed back at me.

After he took a sip, his face turned serious. "Are you scared?"

"Scared of what?" I asked, trying not to sound nervous.

"Come on, Lex, it's me."

I sat down on the couch and took the bottle back. I took a long swig and sighed. "I can do this. I've been training my whole life."

He looked at me. "That's not what I mean. You're going out there with no one to watch your back. You don't know what you're walking into."

"Fine, I'm a little apprehensive," I said honestly.

"Then why are you doing it?"

I stood up and paced. "I can't stay here. I'm suffocating."

"Oberon at you again, huh?"

I looked at him, surprised.

"Seriously? Everyone knows he's been in love with you forever—it's not like he hides it. Why do you think every guy avoids you like the plague? I mean, you're gross, but that's not the only reason," he laughed.

I picked up one of the pillows and threw it at him. He caught it before it hit him in the face. "Thanks," I said sarcastically. "That's exactly why I need to get out of here."

"So, you're just gonna up and leave me?" he asked in a sad voice.

"How'd you find out I was leaving anyway?"

"There are spies everywhere," he said in a fake scary voice.

I raised an eyebrow.

"Fine. Oberon came to me, wanted me to watch out for you."

"You're not coming with me," I said.

"That would never happen. Not if Lana has anything to say about it."

He held out his hand and I reached out and grabbed the gold coin in his palm. I turned it over and scrutinized it. A name was etched into the face: The Café Bar.

I looked up at him. "What is this?"

"It's from a bar in Plaka. You'll find my contact there."

"Your contact?"

He was quiet. "I was sent to Plaka to track down a lead on Zeus. The owner of that bar…helped me when I needed it."

"When did you go to Greece?"

"It was my first assignment."

"Why didn't you tell me? We tell each other everything!" I was amazed that Marius had kept this from me.

"Oberon didn't want me to. Your fascination with the human

world had become obsessive. It was to the point that he feared you'd get lost in your head and forget everything else."

"You still should have told me."

"I'm telling you now. With you gone, who am I going to spar with when I'm having trouble dealing with domestic life?" he asked.

"Oh please, Lana is more than capable of keeping you in check," I said.

Lana was Marius's wife, they'd met when we were all in training. They'd married a few years later and had a baby girl named Jazzbella—or Jazzy, as I called her. In training, we'd been taught that emotion got you killed, and that nothing was more important than the mission. Domestic life didn't resonate with me. I'd never wanted a family—it was easier to be alone. Seeing Marius as a dad was odd—besides myself, he'd been the best assassin Oberon had, but it was good that Marius was starting to settle down. When he met Lana, he had changed. He wasn't the hard-core assassin I had come to love like family. He'd gone soft. I didn't want that for myself, I didn't want to be vulnerable. Sure, Marius was still handy in combat, but when you're protecting those you love, you get sloppy. That's one reason he'd quit a few years ago—Lana got pregnant and he lost his edge.

"Speaking of Lana, if I don't get home, she'll kill me."

He got up from the couch and the smile fell from his face. This wouldn't be easy for either of us. He walked over and wrapped me in a tight hug. I felt his breath hitch, then he pulled back and stared at me.

"Just...don't get yourself killed."

Coming from Marius, that meant "I love you." I leaned in and kissed him on the cheek. Before he left, he handed me a small, translucent device the size of a quarter. I looked up at him, confused.

"It's called a Spyder Cell. Attach it to your neck and you can call me anytime. It's translucent, so it's hard to detect. Make sure you use it."

As I saw him out, I told him to give Lana and Jazzy a kiss for me. When he turned to leave, tears welled in his eyes. I shut the door behind him and retreated to the couch.

I didn't pack; everything I needed for a mission was always ready to go. *This just might be the last time I'll be here*, I thought. *What would I face or find?* I was nervous. I'd heard many things about the human world, I'd watched it since I was young—and now I was about to experience it for myself. What could be more exciting? I couldn't sleep: my mind raced and my hands shook with adrenaline. I was riding a major high. The clock on my microwave read one o'clock in the morning I picked up the wine bottle...empty. Marius had finished it off before he left. What a sweetheart. I crawled back in bed and stared at the ceiling. I hadn't stopped to think about what I was getting myself into, and I didn't care, I was about to start a new adventure. I closed my eyes and drifted into a dreamless sleep.

MORNING CAME HARD AND FAST. My coffee maker sounded off, waking me up.

I wanted to make sure I'd blend in. I opted for dark fitted jeans, a white shirt, and a black tank. I put on my black boots and walked into the kitchen. Pouring my coffee into a large mug, I headed out to my balcony overlooking the ocean. The morning sunrise peeked over the horizon, casting a luminescent glow over the still water. I had the best seat in the house. I've always loved watching the sunrise; it's like watching the world wake up. It makes you feel that for just one moment everything is perfect—too perfect, like my life in Avalon. Maybe I needed a little bit of chaos...but I guess I should be careful what I wish for.

I wanted to be alone when I passed through the barrier separating Avalon and the human world. It's a very intimate process —like part of you is being caressed by the most experienced lover who then grabs ahold of your soul and rips it from your body. Not the most pleasurable of experiences. Oberon, Lucian, and the Sikarios were the only beings in Avalon who could access the barrier. Oberon was pretty controlling, he didn't want just anyone coming and going through the portal.

I stood in front of the barrier, pondering my next step. I'd gone over my trip to the human world in my head so many times. My life would change, but was I ready for that? I stepped up to the barrier. It moved when I touched it, like a ripple in the ocean. It was beautiful. Some people who've been to the other side had wonderful experiences, while others thought it was the worst decision they had ever made. They found the human world full of hatred and deceit...but everyone experiences new things differently. This was the beginning of a whole new chapter in my life and little did I know how much my life would change. As I cautiously stepped through, I whispered to myself, "Here goes nothing."

2

There are moments that teach you to open your heart and feel. Moments that cause you to stop and see everything around you in a different light. Greece was incredibly beautiful. The stone sculptures loomed magnificently. For such a ruthless creature, Zeus sure knew how to be worshiped. I was frightened and exhilarated as his beautiful eyes bored into me, like he was memorizing every detail of my being. I shuddered—would I actually come nose-to-nose with him? It was evening, the stars shone brightly. Time passes differently in Greece, I realized. *Whatever hole you're hiding in,* I thought, *I hope you can see me. Know that I bring your demise.* I would rip his heart out before he could take his last breath. A devilish smile formed on my lips. I felt that cold place inside of me, the place that holds my darkest desires. Sometimes it scares even me. Oberon told me it had manifested after my parents were murdered, sort of like an alter ego. Right now, it called out and I was ready to exact my revenge.

Soon.

I needed to find a place for the night, or for however long it took me to find and kill Zeus. Not that I was in a rush to get back. I wanted to take in as much as I could, and Oberon's marriage proposal lingered in the back of my mind. It was frustrating that, despite my refusal, he still hoped I'd change my mind. It was like having an annoying voice in my head that wouldn't shut up. What would it take for him to finally get the damn picture?

I walked out of the monument and looked down the mountain. I wouldn't make it to the bottom before the sun rose. I took a deep breath and closed my eyes, concentrating on everything around me. I took in the grass at my feet and the warm breeze caressing my skin. Marius said his contact was in Plaka at The Café Bar. Marius said he trusted her. I needed to meet her myself before making that call. I came up with a cover story: I'd be a college student from the university looking for a missing friend.

Flashing was the fastest way to get to the bar.

I remember the first time I tried to flash. I was concentrating too hard on not screwing up, and I found myself on the bottom of the ocean. I was told I needed to concentrate harder on where I was going. In this situation, where I was going was somewhere I'd never been.

I'd have to wing it and pray I ended up where I needed to go. Flashing was like speeding through a small tunnel; it only took a second to get anywhere. It was dark as pitch when my feet touched solid ground—old cobblestone. I looked around and saw I was standing in an alley behind a bar. A noise caught my attention. I slid into the shadows as the back door flew open. A man stumbled out, bent over and retching. He held his stomach with one hand and the doorknob with the other.

You can thank Dionysus for that one.

I stood still as the man wiped his mouth with his sleeve, then stumbled out of the alley, where I'd just seen a car whoosh past. I ran after the drunk and reached him just in time, pulling him onto the sidewalk just as a second car careened around the corner, nearly hitting us. The driver honked and yelled out the window, shaking his fist. The drunkard looked up at me with a bright smile and slurred... a thank you? Maybe.

"Michael! What on earth is wrong with you?!" a woman behind me screamed. I turned as she came storming out of the bar. She was by no means a dainty woman. Her curvy figure sashayed as she got closer, her breasts bouncing with every step. When she stopped near me, the pitch of her voice instantly changed.

"Thank you so much. Sometimes the regulars can get out of hand a bit."

I smiled at her. "No problem."

A good-looking man from the bar walked over to us; he radiated power. He struck me as familiar, but where would I have seen him? Dark hair fell over his indigo eyes. He smiled at me with genuine softness, helped Michael to his feet, and escorted him back to the bar.

"Thanks, Dem!" the woman called after him. Dem raised his hand in acknowledgement.

"Wouldn't it be better to just take him home?" I asked.

The woman let out a musical laugh. "We've already got a cab on the way. My name's Jeniva, but you can call me Jen."

I tried to act calm. Assuming I'd flashed to the right place, this might be Marius's contact. I took her hand and shook it gently. "Lex."

"How about you come in for a drink? Tab's on me."

I checked my emotions as we walked through a door that read "The Café Bar." Based on the outside, I would never have imagined how beautiful the interior would be. The bar smelled old, like a welcoming musk that warmed you, inside and out. The architecture was Old World and masculine, dark with intricate designs. Whoever built the bar had put their heart and soul into it —it was something to be proud of. Everything from the front French doors down to the wooden beer tap handles was planned. A sense of comfort surrounded me, like I was meant to be here. I walked up to the counter which wrapped around the room in a half circle. Chiseled markings of Poseidon taming the sea were carved into the wood. Laughter rang out from the booths lining the wall. The man Jen had called Dem sat with a few women in a booth in the corner. He gazed at me and smiled. The lighting was low, only coming from candles in wall sconces and a chandelier that dangled from the ten-foot ceiling.

I took a seat on the middle stool at the center of the bar. Jen set down a shot glass and filled it with whiskey. I eyed it with curiosity. I had never tried the hard stuff—this would be interesting. I sipped the proffered drink gingerly, moving it around on my tongue. It burned like liquid fire as it traveled from my throat to my stomach, making me cough. The strong aftertaste settled on my tongue. *I'm going to like this.*

"The trick, love, is to take it in one gulp," Jen laughed.

I took Jen's suggestion when she poured me another shot. The smooth whiskey warming me.

"I can tell you're not from around here," Jen said.

"What makes you think that?"

"I know everyone in this neighborhood. Even the university students," Jen smiled.

There goes my cover story.

"She's definitely not from around here," said a seductive male voice from behind me.

The man sidled up next to me and took a seat, looking at me with silver eyes that could drive a woman to drown. I either wanted to move closer to him or run out into the street. I'd soon learn the former would have been the better choice.

"I'm Raider," he said.

A nickname? Maybe something he gave himself?

"Lex," I responded.

"Where're you from, sweetheart?" His voice was as smooth as silk.

Jen returned, saving me from having to answer. Something

about Raider creeped me out. Not in a stalker, weirdo kind of way, but...there's something dangerous there.

"Do you know of a place I can stay for a few nights?"

"Only a few nights?" Raider inquired.

"I'm just passing through," I said.

"Up the road a bit is a bed-and-breakfast called Palladian Home," Jen said.

I thanked Jen for the whiskey as she turned to help a customer. I sat for a moment. Why had Oberon sent Marius here? What was his connection to Jen? I rose from the stool, and a hand gently touched my shoulder from behind. I spiraled around instinctively, knocking off their hand and wrapping mine around their throat.

That was a huge mistake. I swear I heard Marius's pissed-off voice: *Don't draw attention to yourself.* Assassin rule number one. I threw up an invisible barrier so no one would see me holding a bar patron by the throat. I looked up at my assailant: Raider. His eyes were wide with surprise and excitement—not the reaction I expected from a mortal. I expected fear, at least. Interesting. I jerked my hand away and the bar came back into focus, but Raider kept staring. I wasn't willing to hang around to find out why.

I walked out of the bar and down the street, maintaining a casual, but purposeful pace. My skin prickled with danger; I was being followed. I kept walking, but that cold place inside me screamed to be let loose; it fed on my fear. It was ready to protect me no matter the cost. If I didn't calm down, it would take over. I slipped into a side alley by the bed-and-breakfast, sinking into the shadows. Raider stepped into the mouth of the alley, his silver eyes twinkling in the darkness. He scanned the alley for me, but I kept quiet. He stood waiting for a few moments. I was oddly curious about my stalker, but I'd cross that bridge when I came to it.

Palladian Home looked more like a small hotel than a bed-

and-breakfast. It stood three stories tall and the lights on the front of the building provided a soft glow. A mountain towered in the background, adding to the beautiful scene. I walked through the front door and noticed a warm fire burning in the fireplace in the corner. It was homey, inviting. A woman in her mid-sixties sat behind the counter.

"Good evening, dear. How can I help you?"

I wasn't sure how long I'd be here, so I told her I needed a room for a few weeks. She had me fill out the guest registry and gave me the key to my room, pointing up the spiral staircase to the second floor. The room wasn't as small as I'd feared. It was furnished with a full bed, two nightstands with lamps, and a vanity set against the wall. The bathroom was to the left. I walked over to the window, pushed the curtains aside, and looked out. It was beautiful. The cobblestone streets below glowed a silvery blue in the moonlight. Twinkling lights from open businesses danced like flickering candles. I closed the curtains, stripped down to my bra and panties, and got into bed.

I tossed and turned all night; there was too much on my mind. Dreams took hold.

I was ten. I had spent all day down at the cliffs, diving with the other kids; something my parents always forbid me to do. I was coming home, and when I walked in the door the scent of blood hit my senses. Then I saw my parents, lying motionless in a pool of red. Their throats had been cut, their bodies splayed open like a book. Someone lingered inside the house and I ran in the direction of the intruder. I was getting closer. I turned the corner and saw...

I woke up in a cold sweat, breathing hard. I'd had the same nightmare every night since they were killed. I could still smell the blood. Many years have passed, a few centuries maybe, but it always feels like it happened yesterday. I closed my eyes again and fell into a dreamless sleep at last.

The morning sun shone brightly through the crack in the

curtains, landing directly on my eyes. I rolled over, covering my head with the pillow—it didn't help. I groaned, groggy from lack of sleep, but knowing I needed to get up. I had a long day ahead. I wanted to visit Zeus's temple. I wanted to look my enemy in the eyes. Jen was probably a better source for the information I sought, but something told me to visit the temple first. I wanted to know how Zeus escaped from Tartarus without being seen. Did someone help him? I suspected a God, one loyal enough to help him in his vicious crusade to terminate mankind. My mind wandered to Raider, the guy I met at the bar. He was different, for sure.

I threw the sheets off the bed and set my feet on the floor. I wasn't about to walk around in my bra and underwear. With a quick thought, dark jeans, a blue top, and black boots covered my body. A pretty cool trick and very convenient. I locked my room and headed downstairs. Behind the front desk an elderly gentleman sat reading the paper. He regarded me with a smile and watched as I walked out onto the busy streets of Plaka.

The sun shined bright through a semi-cloudy sky. Shops were beginning to open as eager customers waited in line. The smell of freshly brewed coffee traveled from open doors. One day, I imagined I would sit in one of those cafés and savor that rich flavor. That was not my life right now, though. I needed to keep my head on straight and stay focused. I ought to have flashed at the hotel, but I wanted to stand in the busy neighborhood and take a moment to breathe—I might not get another opportunity for a while. I ducked behind a building and flashed.

3

*Z*eus's temple was more beautiful than I cared to admit. Handpicked flowers were placed carefully in vases and set lovingly around the stone sanctuary. Humans crouched down on their knees to pray for a better life. They prayed for their crops to grow, their cows to give more milk, and for their businesses to thrive in a starving economy. *No matter how ardently they ask for help, it won't come*, I thought.

As I approached, I noticed a few men and women packing up to leave. One man stood under the columns of the temple staring up into the heavens. His offbeat demeanor stood out. I watched as he paced and threw his hands up in the air like he was arguing with himself. I approached him slowly so as not to startle him. He mumbled to himself.

"Give me a sign, tell me what to do."

This was interesting. Either this guy was a hopeless worshipper, or a valuable asset. We were alone. I walked up behind him.

"Hey," I said. He whipped around, his eyes erratic.

"Who are you? What do you want?" he snapped.

He was young, maybe eighteen, and exhibited no fear. He

looked like he was losing his grip—I'd have to approach this slowly.

"You really think he can hear you?" I nodded up to Zeus.

"I know he can. He chose me."

Okay... "Chose you for what?"

He glared at me. "I'm not saying a damn thing."

This was getting me nowhere. "You're probably just an obsessed follower," I said. He didn't like that very much and lunged at me. I grabbed him and flipped him over on his back. I allowed him to get up and he lunged again. I flashed behind him, pulled out the dagger in my boot, and held it to his throat.

"Now, what is your connection to Zeus?"

"What's it to you?" he growled.

"I want to know where he is." This was becoming a hassle.

"Why?"

"I have my own reasons." He was silent. "Kid, don't make me force you."

The kid grabbed my hand holding the knife and moved it across his throat, slicing his neck. He fell to the ground. I crouched down and placed my hand over his open throat. His blood spilled through my fingers and dripped onto the grass. He started to gurgle, his blood pooling into his mouth. He tried to say something, so I leaned in.

"This is just the beginning," he mumbled. Then he was dead.

"Dammit," I said out loud. What the hell did that mean? I wiped my blood-covered hand on the grass. I heard a noise behind me and turned around to see a dark figure disappearing in a puff of black smoke.

Perfect, an audience.

I picked up the body and set it behind Zeus's statue. Hopefully it wouldn't be seen right away. I walked over to where I'd seen the dark figure outside the temple and bent down, tracing the indentation of unearthed ground. I'm not sure if the kid had any viable information. Guess I'll never know. Does this complicate things?

I stretched my senses and when I inhaled, a scent I didn't recognize filled the void. It smelled earthy, then turned into a slight musk. I searched the area to see if there were any other onlookers. Thankfully, the hill was deserted. The only things around me were stone sculptures, green hills, and flowers. I walked back over to the dead teenager and remembered how, after my parents' death, all of Avalon watched as their bodies were burned and sent up to the stars. Human traditions are strange. On Earth, flowers adorn graves and sentimental words are carved lovingly into blocks of stone. Why? Will the person lying dead in the ground read those words? Smell those flowers? Is reminding yourself that a person is gone every day a way to eternally remember them? Humans hold onto the lives of their dead like their last living breath. I may mourn the loss of my parents, but I don't dig in the dirt and throw their bodies down into the holes.

I focused again on the task at hand. I remembered Oberon saying something about the Old Ones returning. Did Jen know them?

The morning hours were slipping by. I walked down the hillside and through a park that extended for miles in either direction. The spring weather made me whole; the trees were newly green and flowers were just beginning to bloom. Beautiful marble fountains were spread sporadically throughout the vast plane.

A dozen or so people were gathered in a circle twenty-feet to my right. I proceeded to the crowd cautiously. I looked over the shoulder of one bystander and peered down at a half-naked woman sprawled out on the ground. She was considerably pale. Her lips were blue and her eyes were wide open and cloudy, staring up into the sky. Her neck had been broken, almost ripped off. Blood seeped out of her nose and eyes, soaking the grass beneath her. I almost walked away. This was a human matter.

A smell hit me before I had time to turn around and leave. I inched closer to get a better read on it. It was not human; this was like lilac and jasmine mixed with exotic passion fruit. The smell was very familiar, like something I had been around my whole life. Sirens blared in the distance and the crowd turned toward the sound while I ducked in for a closer look. Behind the woman's ear, as clear as day, was a tattoo the size of a quarter. Three diamonds connected like a triangle: the symbol of the Gods. According to the stories from my childhood, the Gods would sometimes visit Earth. They were always envious of humans because they had something the Gods didn't: mortality. Certain humans who belonged to the Gods would brand themselves with their symbol. Who had she belonged to?

I recalled the dark figure at the temple. Had that been her killer? What was she doing here? Who was she? Was she connected to Zeus? I slipped away from the crowd before the police had a chance to interrogate me. It was time to talk to Jen. How much did she know about Marius? What had he been doing here? I ducked out of sight and flashed to an alley down the street from the bar.

The neighborhood of Plaka was busy; shops were open and cars were out and about. The late afternoon sun was warm, counteracting the chilly breeze. Raider had apparently been standing nearby and stepped in stride with me. I glanced at him but kept walking toward the bar. He grabbed my arm, forcing me to stop. The change came over me; that cold place inside me was ready to take his head. It was like a whole other side of myself arising from the ashes. My body hummed, it saw Raider as a threat. I looked at his hand around my arm and then at his face.

"Let go."

His eyes turned black as night as he glared at me. "I don't know what you are, but it isn't human."

I tried to pull myself out of his grasp, but his hand tightened around my arm. "I don't have to explain myself to you," I hissed.

"You do when you're in my city," he growled back.

"Is that a threat?" I snapped.

His smile was all teeth. "Call it friendly advice."

He left me standing in the street, cutting me off by walking away, no time to rebut.

Perfect, I'm here for two days and already I have a target on my back.

I'm stubborn. I don't let anyone tell me what I can and can't do; I stick my feet in the ground and sprout roots. Marius used to tell me my personality would get me in trouble one day. I'd argue with someone to the death, even after. I got myself to calm down, shifting my thoughts to Marius. I didn't understand why he wouldn't have told me about Oberon sending him to Greece. I hoped Jen could fill in the gaps. How well did I know Marius?

The bar was packed from front to back. The high-backed booths were full of patrons laughing and clinking glasses. The stools at the bar were just as busy. Jen noticed me walk in and nodded. I looked around to see whether Raider was there and sensed him behind me, like death coming to collect on a contract. I resisted the urge to turn around, to acknowledge that I'd clocked him watching me. Later, I'd realize that he would always be watching me.

The man from the other night, Michael, got off the bar stool he had been occupying and offered it to me with a flourish. He smiled broadly, and I had a hunch he would put me on a pedestal for the rest of his life. I watched as he headed off to the other side of the bar.

Jen walked over and poured me a shot. Drinking probably wasn't a good idea, but after the morning I'd had, I deserved it. So many questions were flying through my head that I was having a hard time keeping it all straight. That damn kid killing himself. What the hell did he do that for? What was he talking about: *This is just the beginning?* Beginning of what? And what about the dead girl near the temple? The tattoo on her neck indicated that she belonged to a God, but which one? Why was she killed? The fact that her body was near Zeus's temple gave me an idea of who she belonged to, but why was she there in the first place? If Zeus had killed her…well, that's another reason to take his head.

"You all right, love?"

I looked up from my glass and saw Jen's worried face. She held the bottle of whiskey, waiting for me to accept another drink.

"You can just leave the bottle," I said. I saw her hesitate, then turn around and put the bottle back on the shelf.

"What's going on, Lex? You look like someone just killed your best friend."

I dug into my pocket and pulled out the gold coin Marius had given me before I left Avalon.

"What can you tell me about this?" I handed Jen the gold coin and watched as the color drained from her face. She reached out slowly and took the coin from my hand.

"Where did you get this?" she asked without meeting my eyes.

"A friend gave it to me." I paused. "I believe you know him. Marius."

Her demeanor changed. She scanned my face, reading my body language and emotions to see if I was lying.

"Who are you?" she asked.

"I already told you."

Her defenses were starting to rise. "You told me your name," she said, a little sternly.

"Would you believe me if I told you I'm an assassin from Avalon on a mission from Oberon to kill Zeus before he reclaims the throne and destroys mankind?"

I'm not sure why I blurted it out. Guess I figured if she knew Marius, the rest wouldn't come as a shock. She stared at me, intrigued. She probably didn't expect all of that to come out of my mouth. She looked around the bar, maybe to see if anyone was listening.

"You barely blinked when I said that," I remarked.

"Because I've heard it before, from Marius.

"What was your relationship with Marius?"

"It wasn't like that; our relationship was strictly business," she said immediately. "Marius found out I provided certain services to the Gods. He wanted to know if Zeus was a client."

I had a feeling I knew what those services were. "Was Marius a client?" I asked.

She took a moment, then nodded. Marius's life before Lana was sort of a mystery. He never discussed his parents or whether he had any siblings. When I would try to ask him about himself, he would deflect the conversation with some remark about how I sucked in training. After a while, I dropped the subject.

"I found a dead girl this morning at Zeus's temple. The symbol of the Gods was tattooed on her neck. I know the significance of that brand, Jen."

She got quiet. "What did she look like?" she asked, her voice trembling.

"Fair skin, about five foot six, red hair."

I saw tears pool in her eyes. She turned away from me for a minute, presumably to compose herself. When she turned back to face me, she was trying to stay calm. I noticed her eyes flickered behind me to where Raider sat. Was he part of this too?

"Who is she Jen?"

"Her name's Serene. She was one of my girls."

"Still think Zeus is in hiding?"

"It doesn't make any sense. Why would Zeus come back now? It's been a thousand years."

"That's a question I don't have an answer to. I need to find a man named Akesios. He might be in contact with Zeus."

"I know who he is. He's a client."

Learning that Jen was a madam didn't make me lose my

respect for her. Who was I to judge? I kill people for a living. People do what they have to to get by in life. She sounded as though she genuinely cared for the girls. But it didn't seem plausible. Zeus? A client without her knowing?

"Where can I find him?"

"Last I heard, he was squatting in an abandoned club about ten miles down the road. Lex, there probably isn't a person in Greece who hasn't heard the story about Zeus being overthrown and his promise to return. Many believe it's true. Others think it's just an old story."

Just then, Michael walked up behind me and set his empty glass down in front of Jen. "It's a true story. A great battle a thousand years ago, Gods fighting other Gods. If the rumors are true, and it begins again, we're all fucked. There are also rumors that the Old Ones have returned to find Zeus and return him to Tartarus," he said.

I looked at Jen. She filled Michael's glass and he walked back to where he'd been sitting.

"Greece is unique," Jen started. "It has its legends and its secrets just like every place in the world. The story of the Old Ones has been around just as long as the story about Zeus and the battle a thousand years ago. To be honest, I believe it's true that the Old Ones have come back."

"Where do you think they are?"

"There is an old castle about twenty miles outside of Plaka. Some say the Old Ones lived there thousands of years ago. Who knows? Maybe you'll find the bogeyman up there."

When I'd first walked in, the music had been loud and impossible to understand. My mind had tuned it out. Now, the music was softer and more manageable to listen to. I calmed down, even relaxed. There was laughter and joy. I looked behind me and noticed Raider staring at me intently.

"I can't seem to shake my shadow," I said to Jen, nodding to Raider behind me.

"He does that."

"What's his deal?"

"He's been here since we opened this bar thirty years ago."

He looked good for his age.

Jen left to help some customers who wanted to be topped off, yet again. If these Old Ones hadn't been seen in a thousand years or so, did they still exist? First, I needed to get in touch with Marius. I walked out the back door and into the alley, made sure no one was around, and touched the device secured on my neck.

"Miss me already?" Marius joked on the other end.

"Why didn't you tell me your contact was a pimp?" I shot back.

"Uh…correction. Madam," he answered.

"I'm waiting," I said impatiently.

"I was trying to avoid that look on your face."

"What look?"

"The disappointed, frustrated look you get. Besides, it was before Lana and I got together. Did she give you any information?"

"Not much. I did find a dead prostitute at Zeus's temple though. Also, I have a stalker."

"What do you mean, a stalker?"

"His name's Raider."

"Lex, you need to stay away from him. He's dangerous."

"You know him?" I asked, surprised.

"I know of him. Look, the particulars don't matter. Just trust me."

"Don't worry, I have no intention of running into him again."

"Good. Just be careful."

"I've gotta go," I said, and with that, I hung up. I didn't tell Marius everything Jen had said, I wanted to see if she was telling the truth for myself. I'd visit the club next and talk to Akesios. This was a walk in the park.

I'd learn later how wrong I was.

The streets were alive with sounds and smells. People were outside laughing, music filled the streets, and bistros opened their doors to the warm, inviting early night air. I'll never get tired of this beautiful, ancient, exciting city.

The sense that someone was following me sent my instincts into overdrive. I searched that secret place inside me that was always there, waiting for me to dive in and accept its hand. Sometimes I visit that place when I feel lost or threatened.

Now, the abandoned club was coming into view. The two-story building looked as though it had seen better days. The front entrance was an eyesore, especially compared to the rest of Plaka, with its pedestrian-only streets lined with coffee shops, boutiques, and restaurants, beautiful flowers adorning the balconies. Looking around Plaka is like glimpsing life in a fairy tale. Not here, though. I looked at the entrance to the abandoned club again, the once-neon sign that lit up the entryway hall had stopped working. The sign read "Bely p."

Something ran behind me, a quick *whoosh* twirling my hair around my face. I turned around, but all that greeted me was the amber glow of dying streetlamps. I walked up to the front door, turned the knob, and walked in. The metal door creaked as it opened. A cold breeze passed through me, making my whole body shiver. This might not be such a good idea. The expanse of the room made me feel small, and the dark corners made me uneasy. Was I being watched? Something had run past me outside, possibly the same entity that had followed me before. The wraparound bar, spiral staircase leading to the balcony, and dance floor were all covered in dust and cobwebs.

I found the restrooms at the back of the building. I walked into one of the stalls and then covered my nose immediately as I backed out. Gagging, I left the bathroom to continue my search when suddenly the smell of death filled the air around me. The just-discernible shadow of a large *thing* towered over me. It had to be seven feet tall and its crimson eyes bore down into mine. If

I stared at it too long would it suck my soul out from behind my eyes? It breathed low and quick, a growl rumbling in its chest as it emerged from the shadows. Its hot breath steamed over my face, the ghastly smell like dripping sweat.

My eyes watered—the creature's stench stung like freshly squeezed lemons. It reached for me. I saw dark fur dancing in the wind and a hand with claws that looked to be about six inches long. It wrapped its fingers around my neck before I had a chance to react. I gasped for air and my lungs burned from a lack of oxygen. I grabbed something—a wrist?—and clawed at flesh. The creature wouldn't budge.

The room blurred and my eyes rolled back into my head. It slammed me into the condemned wall by the bathroom door so hard that the wall crumbled to the floor like plaster. I struggled, trying to dip into my secret place to get this thing off me. I screamed, but nothing came out. I kicked the beast between the legs, thinking, *Hard things in contact with soft ones,* a lesson drilled into me when I was a young trainee. Nothing. Balls of steel.

I needed air.

The pressure around my neck loosened and air filled my lungs. A sharp pain shot up my side and I groaned and opened my eyes, registering for the first time that I was now lying on the cold floor.

As I got my bearings and focus, I saw a man grab the creature's head and smash it into the concrete wall. He was almost as tall as the creature, about six foot four and three-hundred pounds of pure muscle. A sense of familiarity made me pause. Where had I seen him before? His eyes met mine. Holy shit. I'd never seen such eyes before—they were crimson, and silver like flecks of diamonds.

Now that I'd gotten a good look at his eyes, I zoomed out and my mouth almost dropped to the floor. If he wasn't a God, he sure looked like one. Flawless light-gold skin, long blond hair pulled back into a bun, and those beautiful eyes. For a moment it looked like black ink spilled into the whites of his eyes. A second passed and they were normal again.

He knew I was looking at him, and he liked it. He moved fluidly in response to the creature; it was like watching a bull and a matador. I figured he must have come up behind us when I was getting strangled.

Just then, the massive creature grabbed the man by the arm and crushed it underneath its enormous hands. The man let out a chilling yell that bounced off the walls, bringing the empty room back to life. I tried to get to my feet, but my legs were limp from my encounter with the concrete. I lay there helplessly, watching as the battle ensued.

Who was this man? Where did he come from? After absorbing a few right hooks, the creature's strength came back at full force. It grabbed the man and smashed his head against the wall. Old brick crumbled as he hit the ground with a grunt. The creature picked him up off the ground and started again. I mustered enough strength to reach into my dark place and throw a bolt of energy from my hand like silver lightning, hitting the beast square in the chest.

The creature threw its head back and roared. It dropped onto all fours, breathing heavily, and turned to face me. As it pushed itself back to standing, I held out my palm and another bolt of silver light struck it in the side of its face. Ecstasy surged through me like a live wire.

The first time I felt that power, I thought I'd go mad. I had so much of it and it was hard to control at first. My trainers were awestruck—they'd only ever seen so much power in Oberon's high council. It surprised me too, to say the least. I accidently caused numerous buildings to explode and started a few wild-fires. It took time, but I learned to calm myself and control the power.

When my bolt hit the side of the creature's face, it let out a loud yelp like an injured dog. I had just enough time to check on the man, who was now kneeling on the ground, before the beast recovered. I crawled over to him—the pain in my legs was horrible, like they had just received a thousand lashes. There was a huge gash on the right side of his head and his left arm was smashed and hanging on by a string. Behind me, the creature stirred, regaining consciousness. If I didn't want to be mauled to death I had to react, and quick.

I considered trying to flash us somewhere else...but we might end up anywhere. That was one of the reasons I hadn't flashed when the creature grabbed me. That, and the fact I was caught off guard. Now, I had to take a chance. The creature rose to its feet, reaching for me. I grabbed the man lying beside me and closed my eyes. The creature lunged the second we disappeared.

4

Sometimes, if my mind is too distracted when I flash, I can end up where I don't want to be. Once, I flashed into my parents' bedroom while they were having sex. To say it was traumatizing would be an understatement. And that's exactly how I felt now, with no idea where I was or where I was going. My barely conscious passenger was no help. I flashed to the hill outside Zeus's temple—didn't think I'd be back here so soon.

"Fuck me," he groaned.

He was lying on his stomach, straining to push himself up to his knees. I watched his muscles flex as he moved and imagined what he looked like under his black shirt. He was perfectly chiseled, like marble. He lifted his head and took in the surroundings, then got to his feet and inspected his arm. It had already begun to heal—he wasn't a man, but something else entirely. Dried blood coated the front of his shirt but it didn't make me recoil. Instead, it brought on a sense of arousal, which honestly, was a little disturbing.

"I'm gonna kill that bastard," he growled.

Obviously, he's well acquainted with the beast. Was there a man under all that fur?

"How's your arm?" I asked.

He smiled wickedly. "Better."

"You're welcome," I said.

He looked at me with curiosity.

"For what?" he said, raising an eyebrow.

"For saving your life," I scoffed.

He tossed his head back and laughed—it was a rich sound. Why was that so funny? Yeah okay, he had pretty much saved *my* life, but if I hadn't flashed, neither of us would be standing here right now. I didn't want to mess with that creature/beast thing again.

"What were you doing back there?" His eyes narrowed. My chest tightened when he looked at me that way. What was wrong with me?

"What's it to you?" I evaded. Don't give up information until he does. "Besides, I could ask you the same question."

"My business is my own. You're in my city and I'm not a fan of outsiders." His smile was all teeth. An image of him using those teeth to rip off my shirt flooded my mind. Okay, this was getting ridiculous.

His intimidation tactics weren't going to work on me. Like I said, I plant my feet. When I was in training, one of my teachers made the same mistake. There weren't many women in the group, so he took it upon himself to make an example of me. Unfortunately for him, it backfired when he tried to catch me by surprise and throw a ball of fire at me. I put up a shield, the ball hit it, and ricocheted back at his chest.

"You're the second person to say that to me, and I'll tell you the same thing I told him. Fuck you."

He closed in on me—so close I got a whiff of the musk and spice scent rolling off him. I struggled to focus on anything other than this ancient cologne, a smell I never wanted to forget. He looked at me warily. He didn't strike me as the kind of man who women stood up to very often—if at all. We didn't say a word to each other, waiting to see who would speak first.

"Is that an invitation?" he asked silkily.

I would have snorted, but I was shocked speechless.

"And if I refuse?" I teased, and something changed in his eyes. For some reason he didn't like my answer. The peculiar way he looked at me almost threw me for a loop. He studied me intently, taking inventory of everything. I didn't get the sense he was checking me out, it was more like he remembered me from somewhere. That same familiarity reared its head again in my mind.

"I will get what I want, one way or another," he said with a hint of playfulness.

He wasn't lying. This sense of inevitability bothered me; maybe because he unnerved me or maybe because I would do anything he wanted me to.

A faint noise sounded in the distance and our heads swiveled as we tried to pinpoint where it was coming from. It drew nearer. The mystery man met my gaze—I registered that his eyes had turned black, and then he was behind me, one arm wrapped underneath my breasts, squeezing almost too tightly. The other arm wrapped around my arms, pinning me to his torso. Dammit. I'd let my guard down to a potential enemy, Marius would kick my ass if he saw this. But it didn't bother me too much; my body was getting a little excited.

His lips were close to my ear and I started to imagine his mouth sucking on it.

"There are a few things you should know about me and you better learn them fast. I do not like to be threatened. If you get between me and mine, I'll tear you apart."

Who the hell is he talking about? If he thinks I'm involved with anything that belongs to him, he's got the wrong person. I tried to shift to give myself air, but he squeezed tighter. Something hard dug into my lower back.

"I'm also one possessive son of a bitch. You get under my skin and you'll never get rid of me."

He licked the vein from the hollow of my neck to my ear, and my heartbeat quickened. What is his problem? Is this some power struggle to keep me in line? Was he pissed off about his conspicuous desire?

"This isn't over, not by a long shot," he growled.

Black smoke twisted and twined into itself, and he dissolved. I had to keep myself from planting my face in the ground. I just wanted to end this whole damn mission and go home.

So that's where the black smoke came from.

I watched as a few humans came walking up the hillside. I had completely forgotten about the kid from the other day and when I got to the back of the statue, my worst fear had come true. The body was gone. Shit. I'd been making amateur mistakes one after another. I was starting to doubt that Oberon had picked the best person to do the job.

I saw a few humans coming closer. I had to get out of there, so I closed my eyes and made myself invisible. In Avalon, no one else had this power. When I tried to ask Oberon why that was, he just dismissed it and said I was very special. And that was that. Being invisible is just as natural as breathing. I watched as the humans walked past me, clueless. They stopped in front of Zeus's statue.

"It's starting again," said a petite woman with long blond hair and gray eyes.

"Darla, you can't be sure," replied her male companion.

"Neither can you. The murders, the disappearances..." Darla said.

"Maybe the kid was killed by a homeless person. You can't just go around digging up old superstitions."

Darla frowned. "Look, Kevin, both of us have seen the prophecy of a second coming war."

I listened quietly. A prophecy? Oberon never mentioned a

prophecy. But Zeus had threatened a second war when he returned to Mount Olympus. How did these humans know all this stuff? I wanted to talk to them, but I couldn't just pop out of thin air.

They stood arguing for a few more minutes and I was about to leave when Kevin said something that caught my attention.

"Maybe the rumors are true and the Old Ones are alive and have the power to stop Zeus."

"That castle has been abandoned for a millennium, there is no way of knowing if they still exist there," Darla said.

"Only one way to find out," Kevin responded.

"After you," was Darla's retort.

Don't mind if I do, I said to myself.

The old castle was just beyond Plaka in a deserted area overlooking the ocean. I hoped I'd find the answers I needed there. It's kind of funny that sometimes, if you want something enough, you can get it. When I flashed, I imagined finding a large castle by the ocean and then I was standing right in front of it. I can sometimes get lucky.

My search for Akesios hadn't turned up anything, but perhaps the man I'd encountered in the abandoned club was one of the Old Ones.

I had to crane my neck just to see the top of the castle. I took the scenic route and climbed one hundred feet up the mountain. I didn't flash because I wasn't sure where I'd end up. Thank the Gods I'm in shape.

The building looked like a castle out of a horror movie. It was made of black brick and shadows slithered across the walls. I almost turned back, but when I reached the twenty-foot fence, something pushed me forward.

I noticed the castle was wired with cameras—one stared right in my face. I'd be discovered eventually and wasn't sure what the reaction would be. It was time to go invisible and snoop around for a bit.

I passed through the gate and walked another fifty feet to the front door. A gravel driveway wound down the side of the mountain. The castle was gigantic; I was a tiny speck against it and I felt a little nervous. I had no idea what the Old Ones looked like or what they might be capable of. I placed my hand on the doorknob and heard it unlock—my own magical lock pick. The entrance opened into a large foyer. Stairs climbed up to a balcony and a hallway to my left led around a corner. The walls were gray stone and covered with tapestries of beautiful gardens.

Would I run into the man from the club? Part of me wanted to —he was gorgeous as hell. The other part of me wanted to stay as far away from him as possible. What was he anyway? And what was that creature I ran into at the club? The Fae lived in Avalon and they were the only beings I knew of besides humans and the Gods. What would happen if the rumors were true and these supposed Old Ones still existed? I didn't know much about them except what I had learned from Oberon.

I snuck up the stairs, remaining invisible so I wouldn't cause an uproar. Just as I rounded another corner, I slammed into something hard. I was knocked to the ground and let out a grunt while stars formed behind my eyes. What the fuck? When my vision came back into focus, I stared up at the man from the club. Oh shit. He looked around frantically, his eyes intense.

I was pulled up forcefully and slammed against the wall so hard that brick crumbled at my feet. In seconds, my arms were above my head and his body was crushed against mine, his face inches away.

I was so shocked, I released my invisibility and appeared in front of him. His eyes widened, then he glared at me, his eyes raking over my body. I'd seen that lingering look before from Oberon, which creeped me out. Not so with this man. His intense stare made my body heat up. A singular nervousness settled in my stomach. I wanted to lean down and suck on his amazingly full lips.

Images flooded my brain: me, lying underneath him, grabbing the sheets while he plunges into me. Him bending down between my legs and sucking on me. His fingers inside me, pumping in and out. I got the uncanny sense that he was experiencing everything I was in that moment. His grip loosened and it gave me the opportunity I needed.

I used the wall behind me as leverage and kicked him in the chest. He let go of me and fell back, hitting the ground hard. He was quick to get up and come after me, but I flashed behind him, grabbed the knife I saw on the back of his belt, and held it to his back. He put up his hands and turned around, facing me. He just smiled. I looked at him, confused.

"Drop the knife," I heard a voice say behind me.

A cold blade stung my throat. I let the knife drop from my hand and it clanged when it hit the stone floor.

"Turn around," the voice commanded.

It was a voice full of hatred and evil. It put me on edge. I turned around, the sword still placed at my throat. Raider. The one person I told Marius I would stay away from stood right in front of me. Also standing there was the man I had seen at the bar: Dem. Raider motioned toward the entrance of the hallway with the sword and looked over at the man from the club standing behind me.

"Nathan, you good?"

Nathan nodded, and Raider looked back at me.

"Move," Raider snapped.

I looked in the direction he was pointing. "Wait, you're not even going to ask what I'm doing here?"

Raider shook his head, anger radiating off him like cheap cologne. "Later," he snapped.

I obeyed without hesitation. I thought about flashing, but I was afraid Raider would kill me before I got the chance. I'd already figured he wasn't human. We walked down the hallway and around a few corners. The smell of blood, sweat, and urine invaded my senses when we descended a flight of stairs to what looked like the entrance to a cave. I stopped so quickly that if Raider hadn't been paying attention, the sword would have sliced right through me.

"Move," he ordered.

"I'm not going down there," I snapped. I began to freak out and that dark place inside me beat against my brain, wanting to get out. What was going on?

"If you don't, I'll throw you in there myself," Nathan snarled. Damn, even his snarl was sexy.

I took a deep breath. I never wanted to beg for my life, but I would not go down those stairs. Why was I freaking out so much? I was scared.

"Look, I'll tell you whatever you want to know, just don't throw me down there."

"Now!" Nathan shouted.

Finally, we reached the bottom of the stairs, ending in front of a cell door. Nathan unlocked it and hustled me in, shutting the door and locking it. Without another word, Raider and Dem headed up the stairs. As Nathan turned to leave I reached through the bars and grabbed his forearm. He turned to face me, and my hand burned like wildfire where I touched him. He didn't flinch and neither did I.

"Please," I said.

He pulled away from me—rather reluctantly, I noticed. It took everything in me not to get on my knees and beg. He walked up the stairs and around a corner, and then I was alone. My head ached, a sharp pain like a six-inch blade slicing through my brain. Something was eating at me, but I couldn't pinpoint why I was so freaked out.

I tried to breathe, tried to focus on something besides my fear. When that didn't work, I closed my eyes tight and rubbed my temples. My body shook. Just fucking great, this is how I'm going out, on the dirt floor of a cage. Oberon would be so disappointed. Hell, Marius would kick my ass if he were here. I could hear him now. *Get the fuck up. You're going to let this beat you?* I didn't contact him. I stood on shaky legs and climbed onto the dirty cot next to me as darkness formed behind my eyes.

I WOKE UP SLOWLY. The cot had turned into the softest, most glorious bed. The air smelled of musk and rain. I breathed in deeply and snuggled into the cot.

Wait a minute. I woke with a start and looked around—I was no longer in the cell. The room screamed masculinity: brick walls and black leather couches sat in front of a warm fire. I lay on a four-poster bed made of gorgeous cherry wood, under a soft comforter covering white sheets.

Where the hell was I? I pulled the comforter back. I was wearing an extra-large gray T-shirt and something hung heavy on my neck. I reached up and felt a thick collar. I yanked at it, trying to get it off. What the fuck! When it didn't budge, I flopped back on the bed, staring up at the ceiling. Why had I taken this stupid mission? It's caused me nothing but trouble. I felt completely incompetent and stupid; I just wanted to give up. I can't go back to Avalon. I've failed and I can never show my face there, not even to Marius.

Nathan was fast asleep in a chair facing the bed in front of the balcony. The doors to the balcony were open. It'd be an easy escape, but I'd come here for answers and I wasn't leaving till I got them. I quietly searched the room for a weapon and found a small dagger behind the headboard—that's where I would've stashed it.

I wanted Nathan to take this damn collar off, so I leveled the dagger at his throat and kicked the chair, causing him to startle. He rose, but the blade stopped him short.

"Nice to see you're awake and doing better," he said sarcastically.

"Take this off me," I snapped, grabbing the collar.

"I guess a thank you is out of the question?" he snarled.

"Ha," I laughed. "Thank you for what?"

"I could have left you down there, you know," Nathan growled.

I heard a noise outside the door, giving him the opportune moment. He grabbed my wrists and pushed me to the ground. He stretched my arms above my head, straddling me as I struggled underneath him. My body ached for him to touch me; to look at me the way he had earlier. I pushed the thought out of my head.

"Um, you might not want to struggle so much." Nathan smiled.

I immediately stopped. Was that a growl?

"Get off me then," I snapped.

"Promise to play nice?"

I nodded. Nathan rose and held out a hand to help me to my feet. After a moment, I indulged him. Intense heat surged through me as I grabbed his hand, but if he experienced the same thing, he didn't show it. I put the knife on the bed and grabbed the collar around my neck.

"Take this off."

Nathan crossed his arms over his chest.

"A *please* would be nice."

I gritted my teeth. "Please."

Nathan smiled with amusement. "No can-do sweetheart, I don't have the key."

"Argg!" I shouted, silently taking back my desire for him. He made me want to hate him till the day I died.

Nathan let out a rumbling laugh.

Something vibrated and Nathan took his phone out of his pocket and looked at the screen. When I used to watch humans from Avalon, I learned many things about their world. Avalon wasn't much different, except our technology had surpassed the human world. We had engineers developing state-of-the-art technology like Marius's Spyder Cell.

Knock, knock.

"What?" Nathan called.

"Are you decent in there?"

Nathan walked over, grabbed the knob, and swung the door open. Raider and Dem were standing on the other side. I dropped my eyes to Raider's hand and saw that he held the key to my freedom. He walked over to Nathan and handed it to him. Nathan walked over to me and reached his hand out to unlock the collar, then stopped.

"How can we be sure you won't leave?"

"Why on earth would I break in then?"

"Touché," Nathan said.

He reached up and unlocked the collar around my neck. It came off easily and he set it on the dresser next to the bed. This was my chance to get the answers I needed. These three men looked Old Ones-esque, I figured. Or at least they may know where the Old Ones are. I hoped it was the former.

"What is that thing?" I asked, nodding at the collar on the dresser.

"Let's just say it was a parting gift from a dear friend," Nathan answered.

I suspected they had a lot of questions for me, but I had some of my own.

"How did I get up here?" I asked.

Nathan cleared his throat. "When I checked on you, you wouldn't wake up. We couldn't figure out what was wrong, so we brought you up here. Figuring out who and what you are has been a little daunting."

I raised an eyebrow. I was wondering the same things about them.

"We figure you might be part human—want to fill in the rest?" Nathan asked.

I remained quiet. My mother was human. She had fallen in love with my father when he'd been on a mission for Oberon in the human world. My father, on the other hand, was a mix. He never talked much about his heritage, especially when I asked about it. I said as much to my questioners.

Nathan leaned nonchalantly against one of the bedposts. I tried to read his emotions, but he betrayed nothing.

"You're not from here, that much we know," Dem chimed in.

"I'm from Avalon."

Nathan arched an eyebrow. "Avalon," he said, more as a statement than a question.

I nodded. Nathan, Raider, and Dem looked at each other. Was I missing something?

"Kingdom of Oberon?" Raider piped in.

I nodded.

"Just great," Dem started. "Not only do we have Zeus going MIA, now we have to deal with the fucking King of the Weird and Abnormal."

"Watch it, buddy," I snapped. Oberon was my sovereign and even though he made me uneasy sometimes, I got defensive when he was degraded.

"Want to tell us what you're doing in Greece?" Nathan asked me.

"I need to find Zeus."

"Get in line," Nathan said.

"Why?" Raider asked.

"I have my reasons," I said

Nathan looked at me suspiciously. "That doesn't answer the question."

I just shrugged my shoulders.

"What do you plan on doing if you find him?" Dem asked.

I smiled. "Easy. Take his head."

All three laughed in unison; it echoed off the walls. Why was it so funny?

"No offense," Raider continued to chuckle, "but you look like you'd snap in two if I slapped you."

"Give me your best shot," I said.

Raider looked at me with surprise. "This is a joke."

"You think I don't have the ability to take out Zeus, I'm trying to prove that I do."

Raider looked over at Nathan, but he just shrugged. Raider was extremely fast, but I was prepared. Seconds before he introduced his fist to my face, I threw up an invisible wall. His bones crunched. He dropped to the floor, holding his hand to his chest. I grabbed the back of his head and slammed my knee into his face. Dem and Nathan's eyes were as big as saucers. Dem held out his hand to Raider, who slapped it aside. Raider got to his feet, but instead of coming after me he just stood there.

"How did you do that?" Nathan asked.

"I had a good trainer. My job is to anticipate my target's every move and take them out with no evidence linking them to my employer."

Silence drowned the room in a sticky coating.

"You're an assassin." Nathan said it as a statement.

"In Avalon we are known as Sikarios. I'm one of the best," I said proudly. Marius beat me in everything. Even though he'd never admit it or flaunt it in my face, he was the best.

"What are you doing in our home?" Dem asked.

I looked at all three of them. *Sure hope you're what I'm searching for.*

"I'm looking for someone..." I began.

"Aren't we all?" Nathan deadpanned.

"I was told the Old Ones live here. I need to find them."

They were all silent till Nathan said what I'd been hoping to hear. "Well, you found them."

5

_I_ stared at him. In Avalon the Old Ones were revered almost like kings. Powerful, exotic, beautiful like the Gods, and mysterious. Some say they were forged from fire; others say they were demons who broke ties with Hades because they were tired of his cruelty. Dem broke the silence.

"Should we go downstairs?"

When I was younger, my mother would read to me when I was lonely. One story sort of reminded me of this moment—it was about a girl who followed a white rabbit down a hole and her entire life turned upside down.

Nathan's eyes were on me as we walked downstairs. I tried hard not to look over at him, but my curiosity won.

"What?" I asked.

His eyes bored into mine. It thrilled and unnerved me. What did that say about my personality? There was this constant pull when I was around him, like we'd been important to each other in some other life. Did he sense it too? I wasn't sure if I wanted to find out. What if he did? What would I do?

We reached what seemed to be the entertainment room, based on the massive flat-screen TVs lining the walls, the pool table in one corner, a bar in the other, and the huge black leather couches and armchairs. This room screamed *male* and the testosterone was suffocating. I looked over and noticed that the TV had been left on, broadcasting what looked like the porno version of *Pirates of the Caribbean*. Raider tried to nonchalantly turn the channel, but the TV was having none of it. Nathan tried to hide his laugh with a cough.

"Let's get serious for a minute," Nathan began. "If you want our help finding Zeus, you tell us what you want with him."

"He murdered my parents," I said. Obviously, there was more to it than that, but I wasn't sure how trustworthy my newfound "friends" were. What if they were protecting Zeus? Or helping him?

"We're not," Nathan said

"How did you…?" I started.

"Your eyes say everything," Nathan said.

Was that a compliment? The one thing I never could control were my eyes—deep green with silver accents and wholly outside my powers. This possible weakness, and possible trouble, drove me crazy.

"You want our help finding Zeus, so you can kill him for taking out your parents. No offense, but that doesn't give us much incentive to help you. We have bigger problems than your revenge," Nathan said.

"What do you want with him?" I asked.

"To keep him from retaking the throne, destroying mankind, and restarting a thousand-year-old war. But, I'm sure you've heard that story, being from Avalon," Raider said.

I nodded. "That's the main reason Oberon sent me, but telling me Zeus killed my parents gave me more incentive. Why do you think he's come back now after all this time?"

They all looked at each other. That nagging voice in the back of my mind tried to tell me I should know this. It was like part of my mind was missing. Weird. How would I know what was going on?

"We're not sure. I had a lead on one of his contacts and I planned to ask him that very same question…but then I found his dead body. And his killer," Nathan said, looking at me pointedly. "Want to tell me what happened?"

So he was the dark figure I'd seen at the temple that first day. I looked at him innocently—well, I tried to anyway. The Old Ones weren't stupid, so why not start with the truth?

"I figured Zeus's temple was the best place to start looking for him. Unfortunately, it didn't turn out the way I wanted, and I ran into a problem."

"Did the kid give anything up?"

"I'm not exactly sure," I said.

"What does that mean?" Nathan asked

"He said, 'This is just the beginning.'"

"Do you know what he meant by that?" Nathan asked.

I shrugged. "I have no idea. I honestly thought the kid was delusional." I paused. "Look, we all have the same goals, mostly. It might benefit us all if we work together."

They looked at each other, mulling it over. It would make more sense to have fresh eyes on the problem, whatever they were doing clearly wasn't working. We needed each other, whether they wanted to admit it or not. This perplexing, familiar intuition took hold, like we were all once acquainted in another, forgotten life. But Nathan was different. For some reason I connected with him more than the others. He excited me, but scared me, too—it was confusing…not to mention heart-stoppingly terrifying.

"She's right," Dem said.

Nathan didn't look convinced, but agreed anyway. "Fine, but you're staying in the castle," he said.

I looked at him questioningly. "Why?"

"Forget it," Raider protested—he didn't want me in the castle any more than I wanted to be there.

I crossed my arms over my chest. "What? You afraid I'll slit your throat in your sleep?" I said to Raider, smiling playfully.

He growled.

"Look, I don't care if you refuse," Nathan said, pointing at me, "and I don't care if you don't like it," he said, pointing at Raider. "It's done. Do you need to get your things from the hotel?" he asked.

"Everything I own is on my body."

Nathan gave me a once-over, a small smile crossing his face. The tip of his tongue snaked out and he licked his luscious lips. Holy. Fuck. This man is going to cause me some serious trouble. My body reacted in ways I tried to ignore.

"You can use the spare room across from mine," he said.

Raider snorted. Just great, this is all I needed. An insanely gorgeous man just feet from my bedroom. So many questions swirled through my head. Did he sleep naked? What would it be like to feel him on top of me, touching me, licking me, sucking me until he hit home and slid inside? To wake up next to him? My body hummed with pleasure...until...

"What?" I asked.

Raider and Dem bit their lips, trying to keep from laughing. I noticed Nathan was not amused. He looked a little annoyed and showed a hint of aggression. Apparently, I was not in on the joke and it was starting to piss me off. What was so freaking funny?

"What? What the fuck are you laughing at?" I snapped.

Dem stopped laughing long enough to answer. "Your eyes are glowing."

Raider laughed. "And you're looking at Nathan like you're gonna suck him dry."

Heat flushed over my face—embarrassing! My eyes shine brighter when I'm excited. I wouldn't say they *glow*, but they come close enough, depending how excited I get. I calmed down and tried to change the subject. "So, what's the plan?"

"There's a popular club about ten miles outside Plaka. We're meeting a contact there who may have information on Zeus's whereabouts," Nathan said.

"Who is this contact?" I asked.

Nathan paused. "Hades."

"Hades." I said as a statement.

"You don't believe it?" Nathan asked.

"Why would Hades help you track Zeus?"

"The obvious reason: Hades hates Zeus and would do anything in his power to destroy him," Raider answered. That you're-so-stupid look showed on his face as he spoke. I wanted to knock his fucking head off right there but figured it wouldn't matter anyway. He was a...whatever he was. He was something you had to kill with a magic wand made from the wood of a super-old tree and crafted by an old crotchety sprite/faerie/unicorn who lived on top of a mountain that took twenty years to get to. Hey, it was possible. There are many worlds in the universe that people have yet to explore. Hell, Avalon was one of them. Instead, I smiled sarcastically and pretended to kill him over and over again in my mind.

"When do we start this little road trip?" I asked.

The faster I got this over with, the sooner I'd be home. And with that thought, sadness trickled over me. Even though I had only been here for a few days and was on tricky footing with these men, I'd been enjoying my time here. I'd found a friend in Jen...well, I hoped so...and Plaka had wedged its way into my heart. And Oberon's proposal remained on my mind. I silently hoped this mission would take a lot longer than planned, a sentiment I would come to regret.

"Tonight. Club Olympus," Nathan began.

I laughed. "Olympus—how fitting."

Nathan ignored my sarcasm and continued. "Olympus gets

busy around eleven. In the meantime, there are some ground rules that need to be put down."

"Excuse me?"

"You're not to approach Hades on your own for any reason. You're to stick by my side at all times and not engage in any activity that might put us or any humans in danger," Nathan said.

"Anything else, Dad?" I said sarcastically.

Nathan growled. "This isn't a joke. Hades isn't the type to give up anything for free."

"I won't get in your way; I'll be a good little dog and not leave your side," I said, barking for emphasis.

Dem laughed. Nathan glared at him, so he cleared his throat.

"Can I at least take a shower? I was down in your nasty cellar for Gods know how long," I argued.

Nathan gave me the once-over again, his eyes lingering in certain places that made my blood boil. Holy shit. This man is going to cause me major trouble and I looked forward to it.

"Fifteen minutes," Nathan snapped.

"What is your problem? Ever since I got here, you've been acting like a dick. Also, I have at least thirty minutes of gross on me," I said.

"I don't trust you, regardless of whether we choose to work together. Fifteen minutes or I'm coming in there after you, and trust me, it won't be pleasant."

I was not getting it. One minute he was cordial, and the next he was a complete dick. It was like he was fighting some inner turmoil to view me as an equal and not as an enemy. I dropped the subject for the moment and headed upstairs. Nathan's gaze bore through me.

"Are you sure this is a good idea?" Raider asked Nathan.

"No. But she'll find out eventually," Nathan responded.

Find out what eventually? I was uneasy, and worried that maybe I'd made a mistake by coming here. I'd have to watch my back.

I opened the door to my temporary room and my mouth hit the floor. A dark, cherry four-poster bed sat against the wall and a beautiful white down comforter and white sheets covered the bed. The light-gray couches to my left sat in front of a fireplace, sconces lined the walls, and a beautiful crystal chandelier hung from the nine-foot vaulted ceiling. I walked over to the balcony that overlooked the crystal-clear waters of the Mediterranean. There was a white chaise lounge and beautiful wildflowers in iron pots. It was peaceful. I breathed in the clear air and felt my lungs open. I wanted to contact Marius, but he'd be upset with me for being here. In my defense, I had no idea Raider was one of the Old Ones or that he lived here.

My fifteen minutes were almost up. I walked into the bathroom without looking around, stripped, and got into the shower, turning the water to hot. What was I getting myself into? When I was finished, I walked out of the bathroom half expecting Nathan to be standing in the room. To my disappointment, he wasn't.

To my disappointment? That was a surprise. A part of me was hoping he'd walk in, see me in the towel, rip it off, and take me right there on the bed. I shook my head to knock the image out and walked over to the closet to look at the racks of clothes. Some were a little too revealing for my liking, but I found a dark pair of skinny jeans, black boots, and a royal-blue tank top that I covered with a black leather jacket—why not take advantage of the closet's bounty? Obviously, women came in and out of this castle. I remembered seeing Dem at the bar surrounded by a group of women.

I let my hair air-dry and went without makeup. I usually ended up sweating it off and luckily my complexion was clear and soft, so I didn't need to wear it. I opened the bedroom door. Nathan stood on the other side, his hand poised on the doorknob. I raised an eyebrow.

"A little late, aren't we?" I said to him.

"Things came up," he responded. "Hades is on his way to the club."

"Do you trust he'll tell you what you want to know?"

"Probably not."

We walked in silence down the stairs. Everyone was gathered in the foyer.

"How do you want to play this?" Raider asked.

"She and I will take the front entrance..." Nathan started.

"My name is Lex," I said.

Nathan threw me a glance, then continued. "Fine. Lex and I will take the front entrance. Raider, you and Dem take the back and move in slow. Hades always has an ulterior motive so watch your back."

6

---

*T*he car ride to the club was quiet. We all piled into the Cadillac SUV and I turned my head and looked out the window. Every now and then I noticed Nathan glancing at me in the rearview mirror. What did he see? I'm sure he still had questions, and he didn't trust me, but I felt the same. Working together might prove challenging.

The club was only about twenty minutes from Plaka. We parked the car in the back parking lot and filed out. We ran through the plan one more time, then split up, Raider and Dem heading to the back while Nathan and I headed to the front door.

Nathan had said the club was a popular hangout for kids from the streets. The bouncer at the front entrance was so huge he looked like a refrigerator. I glanced over at Nathan. Even though he was a hair shorter, he was much more powerful. One thing was certain: I never wanted to be around Nathan when he was pissed off. *But you have been.* The thought came to me unbidden. Odd.

Get back in the game, Lex.

The bouncer gave Nathan a once-over and shook his head, indicating he wasn't going to let us in. Nathan bristled like he wanted to knock the guy's head off and be done with it. He needed to chill, but I refrained from telling him to "let a pro handle it." Instead, I gave his shoulder a condescending pat and walked around him, whispering in the bouncer's ear while Nathan glared. After a moment, the bouncer opened the door and allowed us in…to the disappointment of everyone in line who'd been waiting for a while.

We made our way down a dark hallway lit by candles, the sound of music thudding in the distance. Nathan's irritation at his failure radiated off him—a humid, wet-blanket sensation that made me uncomfortable. I couldn't take it anymore.

"All right, would you stop?" I said to Nathan.

"Stop what?" he asked, looking at me.

"So, you couldn't get us in and had to rely on a woman. Is that it? Are you feeling like your masculinity is being questioned?"

"What are you talking about?"

"Your annoyance and aggravation is coming off you in waves. It's making me very claustrophobic."

"How can you sense my emotions? Some Avalon faerie trick?" he said sarcastically.

"You said I show everything through my eyes. Well, you show everything through your body language. So, chill out."

"What did you say to him?" Nathan asked.

"Just a little mind manipulation. I showed him what he wanted to see."

"Come again?" he asked.

"Instead of seeing a man and a woman walk up to him, I showed him two scantily clad women," I paused, "and you sliding your phone number down the front of his pants."

Nathan's eyes widened. I continued to walk down the hallway, leaving him frozen in his tracks.

"By the way," I called back at him, "you make a really attractive woman." I smiled.

He caught up to me and grabbed my arm. His eyes turned

black and I pulled my arm out of his grip. "Chill out. It was all an illusion. He was the only one who saw. We got in, didn't we?"

He didn't say anything. The loud music hit me as we crossed the threshold into the building. The vibrations pounded against the walls and goth kids were in the corners making out. Hades would definitely hang out here. His thirst for the young and self-loathing got his rocks off. The place was packed, the walls were painted black, and the only lights in the room were the fluorescent neon tubes at the front where the DJ was. I leaned into Nathan, shouting over the music.

"We should split up!"

Nathan stepped back and stared at me. He probably figured that telling me no would only make me defiant, so he leaned in close and grabbed my wrist.

"Keep in my sight, and keep your mouth shut," he said coolly.

Ah, so he's giving me orders, huh?

I wiggled my wrist out of his grasp. "I can take care of myself. I don't need a chaperone," I snapped. I was getting under his skin and I enjoyed it. I wasn't sure what his relationship with Dem and Raider was—was he their leader? I figured he likes to take charge, but we had decided to work together, and he was starting to break that deal.

He began pushing his way through the crowd, away from me. I sidled along with my back against the wall, scanning the room as kids jumped to the hard-rock music and gyrated on each other. I almost got knocked over a few times. I caught Nathan's eye and smiled—and not to get on his nerves, either! Honestly, I was glad he was watching my back.

They all look like they're having a seizure, I thought to myself as I passed a couple trying to writhe in sync with each other. A soft, not-quite-intelligible voice whispered in my head. It was a little troubling—I don't normally hear voices. I looked around to see who was near me—no one. Nathan had left and...my gaze came to a halt.

Hades stood not ten feet away. His Caribbean-blue eyes stared at me with urgency and I stared back at him, fire burning in my blood and my heart pounding in my chest, trying to escape. Time slowed to a crawl—everyone around us danced in slow motion and a faint sound, like someone calling to me, reached my ears. I started to walk toward Hades like I had a rope tied around me and he was reeling me in.

My entire being was getting pulled from my body. I kept my focus on his eyes, drawing me in. I didn't understand why I was losing control. I heard Nathan's voice, but I didn't care: Hades was calling.

I stopped right in front of him. He was inhumanly beautiful with long black hair that hung around his shoulders. I wanted to reach out and feel the softness of it. His eyes, like blue diamonds accented with glitter, sparkled with radiance and as he stood there staring at me, goosebumps covered my entire body. My four-inch stiletto boots brought me to Hades' slightly curved nose, and he lifted his right hand, tucking a strand of hair behind my ear. His touch made my blood feel like fire and wetness pooled between my legs. I closed my eyes and an image formed in my head. In an instant, it was clear who'd planted it: Hades.

In the image, I was in a room lit by candles with large sconces lining the walls. I lay on a large bed, my hair covering my bare chest. The black satin sheets draped below my waist and I flushed, noticing Hades' chiseled, handsome features. He smiled, his white teeth glowing in the darkness as his canines elongated. He brushed my hair off my chest, and I gasped as he grazed my exposed nipple with his fingers. Bending his head down, he ran his tongue up my neck, then dragged it back down to the nipple he'd just toyed with. I moaned, placing my palms on his chest then around to his back as Hades slid his free hand under my back. His erection touched me between my legs, and he slipped inside.

My eyes flew open. I looked around and I was back in the

club. I felt violated, dirty—like something unnatural had taken my body hostage and planted me in that image. Hades had come closer, his arm gripped my waist, immobilizing me.

Nathan shouted at me from the other end of the club. "Lex!"

Hades pulled me closer. He bent his head down and whispered in my ear. "I can smell your desire for me," he said, his voice smooth as silk.

"Oh?" I breathed.

"Me inside you, pounding into you, making you climax."

He licked my ear, causing heat to rush to my face. We were in public and I felt a little embarrassed, but my breath hitched as a seductive smile formed on Hades' luscious lips, and I came.

He chuckled, obviously sensing my desire for him. "I'm going to like you."

I pushed away from him, aware that my sexual attraction toward him was showing. Nathan was somewhere close, and I blushed sheepishly thinking about the person I *really* wanted.

"There's no need to be embarrassed, Lex." Hades said.

I raised my eyebrow. "How do you know who I am?"

He smiled. "I know a lot about you."

My unease was nowhere near subsiding. Nathan and the others were gone—maybe they'd gotten caught up doing something else—leaving me here to deal with this walking orgasm.

"I thought we would meet sooner or later. Personally, I'm glad it's sooner," he said.

I stood quiet. Where the hell was Nathan?

"I want us to get better acquainted. I agreed to help Nathan and the others find Zeus for that very reason."

"I thought you said you knew a lot about me," I responded.

"I meant on a more personal level," he said silkily.

"Help me find Zeus, and I'll consider your request," I said.

"Not part of the deal," he responded.

"You made a deal with Nathan to give up information on Zeus in exchange for me?" I asked, incredulous. Something was off.

What was it about me that had made Hades willing to help? Why was I so expendable? A part of me had stirred in Greece—something that had been hidden in the darkness of my soul.

"Be with me, and I'll give you what you want."

"No." It was a firm statement; I wasn't going to budge. "What do you have that I would want?"

"Answers. To the question you have been asking yourself your whole life."

"What would that be?" I asked nervously. Where the hell was Nathan? This whole exchange was taking too long. Was Hades preventing him from getting to me?

"I know who *really* murdered your parents."

I stopped breathing. "Zeus murdered my parents."

"Wrong," Hades said flatly.

"Who, then?" I snapped.

Hades was quiet.

"Tell me!" I screamed

He smiled again. "Your. Beloved. King."

As Hades said the last word, rage boiled up inside me. I was ready to punch him in the face before someone grabbed my arm.

"What the bloody hell are you doing?" Nathan snapped.

I pulled my arm out of Nathan's grasp and turned to Hades. "You're a fucking liar," I yelled.

I stepped forward again. That dark place inside me was ready to explode. Heat and energy crawled up my arms. Screw all these witnesses—Hades would meet my fist. The God grabbed a boy who'd been dancing nearby, completely unaware of what was happening. Hades wrapped his arm around the boy's forehead and the top of his shoulders.

"I wouldn't do that if I were you," he hissed.

I stopped.

"Good girl." Hades' smile was the definition of evil.

"Let him go," I spat through gritted teeth.

The music got quiet, like it was far away, and I looked around, noticing how Hades had manipulated our surroundings. No one knew what was happening right in front of them—no one except the young boy. It was like we were invisible to everyone else in the room. I saw tears in the kid's eyes, begging me to save him.

"You don't get it, do you, Lex? I'm offering you information, information to help you find Zeus and end this. And you spit it right back in my fucking face." Hades was steaming.

"You expect me to trust you on blind faith. Screw your information," I snapped.

Hades' grip on the boy grew tighter. He was inches from snapping his neck.

"Let the kid go, Hades," Nathan snarled beside me.

"Look around you, Nathan. They're cattle. What the fuck does it matter how they meet their end? I remember you once despised humans," Hades said coldly.

I looked over at Nathan. What was Hades talking about? Nathan's body grew rigid, but his face betrayed nothing.

"You're a coward, Hades," I snapped.

A loud crack echoed through the building. The boy went limp, his face smacking against the floor. Hades winked at me.

"You didn't win this one," he said, and with that, Hades vanished.

Screams bounced off the walls—our shield was gone. People ran to the exits, trying to escape the building, but I stood motionless. I saw Raider and Dem run up to Nathan. They were all talking too fast to understand, but it didn't matter.

"Clean this up," Nathan said to them.

He grabbed my arm and we melted away in a cloud of black smoke. In moments, I found myself standing in Nathan's bedroom, the events of the night and Hades' outrageous story racing through my brain. Oberon, my parent's killer. Did Marius know? Did I miss some telltale sign? I strained to remember, but it was like my memory had been erased. I watched as Nathan paced the room. He was furious.

"How could you be so reckless?" he snapped. His voice echoed off the walls, loud enough to bring the castle down. "Your inability to control yourself cost that boy his life!"

"Do you think I did that on purpose?" I yelled back, balling my hands into fists. If he'd only shut the hell up for a minute and let me explain... "Do you think I planned to lose control?"

"That's just it. *You* didn't think," Nathan snapped. "I told you to stay in my sight, to keep your mouth shut. Our best lead on Zeus just went up in smoke."

"Don't talk to me like I'm a child."

"Then stop acting like one. This is the real world, Lex, you should know that."

I noticed the tone of his voice had changed, the way it grumbled in his throat. He was pissed. Something lurked under that gorgeous exterior and it was pure evil.

"Why couldn't you have just listened? If you'd done what I told you that kid might still be alive."

"You don't own me!" I shouted. He was trying to control me, and it was pissing me off.

All of a sudden, he was so close that our feet almost touched. I hadn't even seen him move.

"That kid's death is on you, so I hope you can live with that. You won't want to." His teeth were clenched.

I pushed Nathan away from me and walked out the door—the castle was quiet, and a light breeze danced inside the hallway. I just kept walking through the endless corridor, finally stopping in front of a massive window that looked out toward the calming ocean and the beautiful stars. Was that kid's death my fault? I thought I could handle the situation on my own. Was that stupid? Why can't I listen? I'm so fucking hardheaded sometimes. And Oberon killing my parents...sickening. Why? Why would he do it? Why would he send me here if I might find out the truth? Maybe he assumed I wouldn't buy it. I swung my arm out and hit the wall, it rattled and part of it crashed to the floor. I crouched down to clean up the mess.

"Please don't destroy our home."

I turned around and saw Dem walking up behind me.

"Sorry," I grumbled.

We stood in silence for a few minutes, looking out at the ocean.

"I really fucked up, didn't I?" I asked.

He contemplated me with a small smile. "Well…it wasn't the smartest thing to do."

I lowered my head and shook it, defeated. I'd played right into Hades' hands and delivered that kid on a silver platter. Dem touched my shoulder. When I looked at him, he reached his hand up and wiped a tear from my cheek.

"It won't be the last mistake you'll make," he said.

"Is that supposed to comfort me?" I asked, incredulous.

"No, it's supposed to make you understand that shit happens. It's how you come back from it that keeps you from making the same mistake again."

"Well, thank you, Dr. Dem," I said.

"You can stand here and feel sorry for yourself as long as you want, or you can pick yourself up and keep moving. We all fuck up. No one in this place is innocent."

Huh. None of them were innocent. I used to be, but my world had come crashing down the day I lost my parents. I spent time distancing myself from everyone—the only way to cope was being on my own. Without Marius, I wasn't sure what would have become of me. I shuddered.

"Thank you," I said with sincerity. Dem was deeper than the others, like he had experienced all the horrors in the world but was able to come out the other side with his soul still intact.

I headed upstairs to shower. I needed to get the remnants of Hades off me. The hot water cascaded down my back. What was I doing here? Was I making the right decisions? Had I gotten in way over my head? I'd already been here for a couple days and I was no closer to finding Zeus. I felt lost, alone, and betrayed.

Why would Hades lie about Oberon killing my parents? What's his angle? How did Hades and Oberon even know each other? What the hell was going on? Before my self-doubt led me to jump off the balcony, the water turned cold. I wiped the condensation off the mirror and looked at the person staring back at me. I didn't recognize her; she was wide-eyed and pale. They always say there is a first time for everything, and that kid back at the club had been my first fatal mistake. I would come to realize that Dem was right; it wouldn't be my last.

I climbed onto the massive four-poster bed and sank into the mattress but my mind wouldn't stop racing. I tossed and turned, the boy's face haunting me. I didn't even want to complete this mission, maybe Oberon had lied about Zeus wanting to destroy mankind.

I got up to venture downstairs, making my way through each room. The kitchen, as big as an apartment with stainless steel appliances, granite countertops, and cherry wood cabinets; the entertainment room; a large office, its walls lined with monitors; and finally, the room I was looking for. There was a large ring in the middle of the room, two hanging bags to the left, free weights to the right, three ellipticals, and three treadmills. Flat-screen TVs lined the wall in front of the machines. I wrapped my hands in tape, stripped down to my sports bra and underwear, and walked over to one of the hanging bags, starting to spar. Right hook—how could I have let Hades kill that kid? Left hook—was Hades telling the truth about my parents? Jab—why the hell did Oberon send me here if there was a chance I'd figure this out? Roundhouse kick—should I still go after Zeus? Uppercut—will I ever know the truth?

Sweat dripped down my back and face—I'd needed this, it helped clear my mind and redirect my focus. I was sent to stop Zeus from destroying mankind and to avenge the murder of my parents. Now, I wanted to find him to learn the truth.

Someone walked into the room: Nathan. I was out of breath, sweat dripping everywhere; I felt disgusting. The look on Nathan's face told me he didn't mind the view. I grabbed a large towel from the nearby rack and wiped my face.

"I couldn't sleep," I said.

"Good. You can help me with something, and maybe redeem yourself in the process."

With that, Nathan walked out of the room. Before he left, he called over his shoulder: "Go clean yourself up and get changed. You've got ten minutes."

"Anything else, sir?" I mumbled under my breath.

I saw Nathan hesitate, but he kept walking. I did what he'd asked, then waited in the foyer. What could he need help with? It was almost three o'clock in the morning and I was standing in a house occupied by three...whatever they were, waiting to see what kind of punishment Nathan had in store for me. He walked down the stairs five minutes later, dressed in all black. I was shocked that this gorgeous man had so much menace to him.

"Where're we going?" I asked when he approached me.

"I have another lead on Zeus," Nathan said.

We walked out of the castle and got into the SUV. I guess this little trip was just going to be the two of us. Great. I buckled my seat belt and looked over at him.

"Why do you think Zeus is hell-bent on destroying mankind?" I asked.

Nathan was silent. "When the Kingdom of Light lies down with divine power, the destruction of man will bring forth everlasting darkness."

"What is that supposed to mean?" I asked.

Nathan flicked his eyes my way, then back at the road. He was quiet for so long it was like he was trying to figure out what to say next.

"It's the prophecy of a second war. The kingdom of light,

Mount Olympus, joins forces with divine power, destroys mankind."

"What is this divine power?"

"I'm not sure, but I think Hades might know. Hence, why we are out here at three in the morning. If I can't get to Hades directly, his right-hand man is the next best thing."

"Nathan, I heard about this prophecy. A few humans at Zeus's temple were talking about it."

"What did they say?"

"They said they had proof of a second war. We need to find them and see what else they know."

"I want to find Hades. He's more connected to this than any human. To find him, I need to find Vic."

"So, what's the plan?" I asked.

"I'm not sure yet."

We sat in silence the rest of the drive. I was out of the loop, but I had to trust that Nathan wouldn't throw me in the fire. He wasn't telling me everything about the prophecy and I wanted to find the people I'd overheard outside the temple so I could question them—even if I had to do it alone.

We drove for at least thirty minutes to a warehouse district outside Plaka. It was quiet and dilapidated. Greece is beautiful, but it's not all enchanting scenery. There's ugliness, too. People can be ugly too, but sometimes—like with Hades—you need to look a little deeper to see it. Nathan parked the SUV a block away from the district, where civilization still thrived, and turned to face me.

"I'm using you as bait," he said matter-of-factly.

My eyes bulged. "I beg your pardon?"

"I need to draw Vic out and you're his type."

"How do you know he's here? Why am I his type?" I questioned.

"I've been tailing him for a few days. This is where Vic usually spends his time, and...you're a woman."

I got out of the car and looked over at Nathan. Vic had better be worth it.

"I'll be watching from the roof over on that building," he said, pointing to a tall, abandoned building that sat back behind two shorter ones. Between the two was a dark alley—hell, every alley was dark. I turned around to ask him where I should wait, but he was already gone. This would be a long night.

7

J sat in the alley waiting for Vic. What did the prophecy mean? How did Hades fit into it all? And Zeus? Large dumpsters lined the brick walls of the old buildings and the air was cold and still, though a slight breeze rustled the fallen leaves on the cobblestones. I made myself as comfortable as I could, sitting on a few boxes and waiting alone in the dark as the night got colder. I was getting a cramp waiting for this asshole, so I stood and looked around. I'd left the comfort of a royal life to play in squalor with low-level creatures.

A soft, uneasy breeze blew into the alley and the streetlights grew dim. I noticed something creeping in the shadows. As corny as this sounds, the smell of death hit my nose.

"Vic," I whispered.

His scent was close, his breath cold on my neck. An arm wrapped around my waist, while another reached across my shoulders to grasp my neck. The fingers tightened around my throat and I gasped. Vic put his nose to my neck and took a deep breath. I tried not to gag as Vic glided his hand from my waist to the inside of my thighs. Who the hell does this guy think he is touching me like that? If Nathan doesn't get here quick, I'm gonna jump the gun and kill this fucker. Vic had power, but it was nothing like Nathan's.

A figure emerged from the shadows and stepped into the moonlight. I recognized Nathan without seeing him—his scent was warm and comforting, like home. *What a weird thought.* I cleared my head and focused on what was happening here and now. Vic's grip grew tighter as Nathan approached.

"Nathan. It's been too long, my friend," Vic hissed by my ear.

"Let her go, Vic."

Vic inhaled deeply against my neck. I jerked, but his grip was too tight. "I smell power in you. It's intoxicating. Such a shame to let a beautiful creature go to waste," he purred.

I'd been sitting in trash while waiting for him, and he was commenting on how beautiful I was? He must have a twisted sense of beauty.

As Vic spoke, Nathan stepped closer.

"One more step, Nathan, and I'll tear her pretty head off."

Nathan stopped and held his hands up as he stepped back.

"I knew he would never put you in danger. He's so protective," Vic whispered in my ear.

He pulled my hair aside to expose my neck. His eyes were fixed on Nathan, completely oblivious to the closer threat, the one in his own arms. He had no idea what was about to happen.

"Therein lies your first mistake, Vic," I said. "Thinking I was the one in need of protection."

In a flash, I was behind Vic. He was so surprised that he didn't notice the six-inch blade I'd shoved into his back. I kicked the back of his knee, causing him to fall forward onto the ground.

"I should have killed you," Vic wheezed.

"That would've been smart," I replied.

Vic tried to bite my leg, but I dodged just in time and kicked him in the face. I looked up at Nathan. "Why did you bring me here? You could have done this yourself."

"I know. I thought it would help get your mind off what happened last night."

"By using me as bait?" I wasn't mad, just curious what his answer would be.

Nathan just shrugged. I figured he didn't have a good answer.

"Now what?" I asked.

"We'll take him back and find out where Hades is, maybe even Zeus."

It was dark now that the streetlights had dimmed, with the only real light coming from the full moon. I watched as Nathan ran his fingers through his hair. I hoped one day it would be me he was running his fingers through. That was an unexpected thought. The more time Nathan and I spent together, the more I wanted him. His emotions were all over the place. Sometimes he seemed to want me, then he'd look at me like I repulsed him or even scared him.

Nathan bent to pick Vic up off the ground. I turned toward the car and stopped short; we weren't alone.

I wasn't certain what our company was, but there were three of them. The two men had distinct tattoos—one had a lion that wrapped around his neck, the other had a dragon slithering from behind his ear—and the third was a woman. They stood silent, unmoving. Was my mind playing tricks on me? The silence lifted when the man with the lion tattoo acknowledged Nathan who was behind me. His teeth sparkled like fresh snow in the moonlight when he smiled.

"Drop him, demon," he hissed at Nathan.

"If you want him, come and get him," Nathan replied.

The man growled. "How about a trade? You can keep Vic, and we get her in exchange."

Nathan advanced his step. "I'll keep them both and you can suck it, Lance."

I wanted to tell Nathan I had this, but the look on his face made me change my mind. Something dark and unnatural clouded Nathan's eyes. Whatever was inside Nathan was clawing to get out. Lance stopped smiling; we weren't getting out of here without a fight. Nathan may have sensed my anticipation, which reeked like cheap perfume.

It all happened in a blur. Lance and I launched toward each other. When we collided, I flashed. I didn't want to go far—even though Nathan was tough and capable, it seemed wrong to leave him—so I kept my mind on the alley. The fucker grabbed hold of my hair—seriously, my hair?—when we materialized and punched me hard in the jaw. It hurt, but I recovered quickly. As he readied himself to dole out another blow, I turned my body, kicking him in the face. He fell to the ground and I slammed my boot heel into the back of his head. Blood and gore, everywhere.

I immediately searched for Nathan and found him to my left, holding his own. Someone ran up behind me—I flashed and watched as Lance ended up running face-first into the brick wall. I pulled his head back and smashed his face into the wall again. Lance threw me into the opposite wall and I fell to the ground. This thing had superhuman strength; one blow and I'd be knocked into the next world.

I didn't have time to flash when he launched his entire body on top of me, pinning me down. I moved to throw him off, but he was one step ahead of me. He grabbed my hands and held them above my head. His weight overpowered me and being pinned to the cold asphalt was not helping. I tried to flash, to call on that cold place inside me, but I was finding it difficult. I glanced over at Nathan, who had one hand around the other guy's neck, and saw that the woman was on Nathan's back, getting ready to sink her teeth in.

I pulled my focus back to my current situation. These things were...I wasn't sure. Demons, maybe, since their faces changed and grew dark, like something out of nightmares. Lance primed himself to take a chunk out of my neck.

Meanwhile, Nathan breathed deeply; his strength was depleting, but he was able to punch the guy in the face and the sound of bones cracking echoed off the walls. The woman extracted her canines and sank them into Nathan's shoulder. He howled as blood rushed down the back of his collar. I watched Nathan reach behind with his free hand and grabbed the woman by the back of her neck. She struggled as he pulled hard, tearing her head off. She burst into flames, disintegrating to ash. The guy Nathan was holding seized the opportunity, grabbing Nathan by the wrist and biting down hard.

Lance's saliva dripped onto my face as he leaned over me; his breath was cold and foul. Goosebumps formed all over my body. I was taking deep breaths, and he looked down at my chest as the sweat pooled. The sweater I was wearing seemed as though it was getting tighter. Lance licked his lips. then traced his fingertips over my breasts. I was struggling ferociously, but this thing was a lot stronger than I was. I closed my eyes tight, my breathing speeding up. I had one last chance while he was preoccupied, and his grip started to slip.

I was able to get my arm free and grabbed his long hair. I yanked back on it so hard he yelped. He struggled to get free, but I held on for dear life. My hand sparked with a power I'd just started learning before I left Avalon, catching his hair on fire. In a matter of seconds, he was engulfed in flames. He screamed, and my other arm was free a second later. I stood and watched as Lance exploded, stepping back to cover my face. I was a little surprised it had worked. Charred parts flew everywhere.

Nathan walked up, clutching his shoulder.

"You all right?" he asked.

I nodded, looking at his shoulder. "I should ask you the same thing."

There was something behind us. Time slowed as a single man stepped into view under a light post. I figured he had been watching the fight from a distance, biding his time. His features were distinct and he was twice as large as the others. His dark hair was slicked back into a ponytail, as black as raven's feathers.

"Ares," Nathan said.

I looked at Nathan, surprised. What was the God of War doing here? Ares smiled, his grin reached to his silver-and-blood-colored eyes. Suddenly, he stood a few feet behind Nathan. How did he do that? It had all happened in a matter of seconds.

That cold place inside spurred me into action and I shoved Nathan to the ground just as Ares raised his arm. The knife he had in his hand sliced through my side. That. Fucking. Hurt.

Intense heat rushed through me, followed by excruciating pain. Poison rushed through my blood and I looked down at my side and watched as blood poured out like water from a faucet. I crumbled on the asphalt with a thud and lolled my head to the side, watching Nathan. His face was met with a right hook. His head jerked to the side; blood splattering out of his mouth.

Nathan gathered himself and was quick the next time a fist came swinging. He straightened and grabbed Ares by the wrist, bending it back as the sound of cracking bones echoed through the alley. Ares screamed, but recovered well, swinging his foot around and kicking Nathan in the face. Then, as quick as the wind, he disappeared.

Nathan crouched down beside me, placing his warm, gentle palm on my cheek. His eyes were worried; they told me I belonged. He glided his hand down to assess the damage and when he gently touched my side, I jerked and gasped. Idiot! I'd come here to redeem myself from the incident at the club and it ended up almost costing me my life.

"Vic?" I wheezed.

Nathan looked over his shoulder, then back down at me. "I threw him in the dumpster over there," Nathan motioned. "He's still alive. I'd like to know why we were attacked."

"Maybe Hades knew we were looking for Vic. I fucked up, huh?" I said.

Nathan shook his head. "This is all my fault."

I didn't argue with him. There was no point, and I was getting tired. Nathan must have noticed my eyes closing, so he lifted my head.

"Lex, you need to stay awake."

I kept my eyes focused on Nathan. His eyes were calming, not dangerous, as he talked to Raider in his cell. I would get shit from him for sure. I hadn't been here for more than a few days and already I was losing confidence in my ability to figure out what was going on. We needed to find Zeus before this prophecy came true. Apparently, Hades was the only one who knew where he was, and Hades had gone MIA. Nathan collected me and I laid my head on his chest. He tensed for just a moment, then he relaxed.

Nathan laid me across the back seat of the SUV. I was starting to lose consciousness, but I heard Nathan throw Vic in the back. The ride to the castle took forever.

"Why can't you just smoke us back to the castle?" I asked.

Nathan chuckled. "I don't want to risk injuring you more."

The SUV stopped. I watched Raider come out of the castle, go to the back of the SUV and take Vic inside. Nathan climbed out, picked me up, and headed toward the house.

"Stop," I said.

"No."

"Nathan, stop."

He sighed.

"Put me down," I said.

Nathan looked down at me. "Why?"

"Just…trust me."

Nathan set me down. As soon as my feet touched the grass, I could feel my strength come back. The gash in my side began to close. Every part of me reached out, grabbed the earth, and held on. Our connection to the earth is what keeps us alive and thriving. Nathan gaped, watching as the color came back to my face.

"You really don't know much about what I am, do you?" I laughed.

He let me stand on my own and I looked up at the night sky and closed my eyes. My lungs filled with fresh air and I became whole again. I started to head toward the house, but Nathan reached for my arm and I stopped and turned to him.

"Where're you going?" he asked.

"To talk to Vic."

"Leave that to Raider. You need to rest."

"No, I don't. I'm fine. I can get us what we need."

He wasn't going to argue. "Raider took him to the cellar."

I tripped going up the stairs as we made our way to the front door. Nathan caught me before my face hit the pavement.

"Are you sure you can do this?" Nathan asked, uncertain.

I evaded his grasp and internally shook off the desire that was rising inside me. Just being this close to him made me want him —the way he touched my arm and looked into my eyes. I didn't answer. I opened the front door and walked in. It was quiet in the castle, a change I found almost unsettling. Nathan walked behind me, quick on my heels. Excited or eager? We descended to the cellar.

Nausea made its home in my stomach—my own time down here was still fresh in my mind and I wasn't thrilled to be back so soon. A single door loomed at the end of the hallway, inviting me to guess what was on the other side. An image of Vic chained to a chair next to a medical table sparked in my mind as Nathan opened the door and stepped aside to let me in.

Well, I hadn't been off by much. Vic sat in a chair, his back to me; Raider was standing in front of Vic, his knuckles bleeding. I looked over at Nathan, my eyebrow raised.

"Vic isn't much of a talker," Nathan said.

"Is that Nathan?" Vic chuckled.

Nathan and I joined Raider. Vic's face looked like a punching bag; it was no wonder they were getting nowhere with him. Vic was obsessed with pain, got off on it, craved the kind of pain that made humans cringe. I could dish out a different type of pain, the type that would get him to talk. Vic stared at me with genuine interest and lust.

"Leave us alone," I said without looking at either Nathan or Raider.

They didn't move. I understood their hesitation, so far, I hadn't given them any reason to trust me.

"We don't really have much of a choice but to trust each other. That is...if you want to work together," I said.

"She can't do any worse," Raider shrugged.

He walked out, followed a few seconds later by Nathan.

"Alone at last," Vic said.

I stood there looking at him. His smile made me feel dirty, like no matter how many times I vigorously scrubbed my body to the bone, I would never get his presence off me.

"Where's Hades?" Straight to the point.

"Ha!" Vic laughed. "Like I would tell you."

"Don't play stupid, Vic. I'll get what I need one way or another," I said.

"Mmm, I knew there was a little freak in you."

I caressed his cheek. I wrapped my fingers tight around his throat and he jerked. A small electric jolt shot from my fingers. The lightning tentacles reached out like a serpent wrapping around the side of his face up to his eyes. He screamed and tried to jerk away, but I held on. After a few moments I let go. Vic looked up at me, eyes as big as saucers.

"Where is he?" I asked.

Vic composed himself but didn't say anything. Defiant little fucker.

"I could do this all night. Can you?" I seethed.

An hour later, Vic was begging me to stop. Well...begging as much as he could with half of his jaw hanging by a thread. He had continued to play games and it was pissing me off. After a while, I started to enjoy inflicting pain. It was satisfying to experience Vic's fear seeping into me. This gratification was new, but I didn't shy away from it. It was only after the skin on the side of his face was so badly burned that the flesh started to slide off that he cooperated.

Nathan chose that moment to walk in. He looked taken aback by Vic's appearance and grabbed my arm to pull me from the room. I yanked out of his grasp, climbed the stairs to the top of the cellar and walked into the foyer. I pushed open the door so hard it smacked up against the wall.

"What the fuck are you doing?" Nathan growled.

He grabbed the door handle and slammed it shut. I stopped and turned to face him.

"It's called an interrogation."

"You filleted him like a fish," Nathan snapped.

"You don't like how I work, be absent next time," I snapped back. "And anyway, you're one to talk. You're a wolf in sheep's clothing."

Nathan was quiet as we stared at each other for a long time, waiting to see who would crack first. We were both conflicted. Some moments it seemed like he was the only person who understood me. Then, in an instant he'd push me away, like being near me disturbed him. When he put up a wall, I returned in kind.

"Did you at least get anything out of him?" he asked.

"Hades' home is sixty miles outside of Plaka in Hydra," I said, walking away.

"Where're you going?" he asked.

But I didn't stop or turn around—I was too tired. I trudged to my room...my borrowed room. I'd depleted a lot of energy with Vic and I needed a recharge. I put on a sports bra and underwear and got into bed. I wanted to contact Marius; I wanted him to tell me if what Hades said was true. I was too scared.

I DON'T KNOW how long I'd been asleep when someone shook me. I blinked awake and saw Nathan's crimson eyes gazing at me. His breathing was deep; he had been worried and was calming himself. I wanted to reach out and caress his cheek, bring his lips to mine, and…

"Lex."

I shook my head. "What?"

"We've got a problem," he said.

I threw the covers back, got out of bed, and pulled on the sweatpants that were lying on the floor; I didn't even bother with a top. Whatever Nathan had been worried about seemed urgent. Nathan froze, staring at me. He raked his eyes up and down, lingering on my breasts. My heart temporarily stopped. My brain stalled, trying to remember that we were going somewhere, before registering what was going on.

"Nathan," I said.

"Sorry," he said quietly.

We raced out of my bedroom and I followed him down to the cellar. Raider and Dem were already there. Vic was in one of the cells, convulsing. I looked up at them, confused.

"What happened?" I asked.

"How the fuck should I know? I came in to check on him and he was like this," Raider said.

"Open the door," I said to Raider.

"Don't think that's a good idea."

"Now!" I raised my voice.

"It's your funeral," Raider grumbled.

He opened the cell door and I walked in and knelt down by the shuddering creature. Vic reached out and grabbed my arm. Something changed in him. My eyes grew wide—this was no ordinary demon. His face kept changing: a vampire, a demon, a man, a bull, a lion. What the fuck? He tried to pull my essence from me, so I threw a bolt at him, but it came right back at me, full force. I was thrown against the wall as the bolt crackled around me. Nathan reached out.

"Don't!" I yelled.

I had to take the ride; it was like a magical high. Vic had tried to manipulate my magic to incapacitate me, but the cold place inside always works with me, never against me. I took a moment to calm down, I'd never felt anything like that.

"Whoa," I breathed.

The guys stood staring. Vic's bolt-redirection attempt had unfortunately backfired; he'd ended up a crispy critter.

"Fuck," Nathan said, rubbing the back of his neck.

"What the fuck was that?" Raider asked.

I stood up. "Well, our friend over there wasn't an ordinary demon."

"What do you mean?" Nathan asked.

"He is able to grab onto the essence of other beings and use it to his advantage; he can use their own power against them."

"Come again?" Nathan said.

"Basically, Vic tried to kill me by using my power against me."

"Why didn't it work?" Dem asked

"Well, we all have our own..." I searched for the word, "signature, if you will, and sometimes those signatures backfire. Depends on the energy."

"So basically, you're a power cable with a kick-ass charge?" Dem asked.

Honestly, I wasn't sure. Vic should have been able to kill me, or at least do the kind of major damage that would keep me off my feet for a few days...or months. I would say I was just lucky.

"Any bright ideas?" Dem asked.

"We know where Hades is, I say we start there."

"Get rid of this," Nathan said to Raider, motioning to Vic's remains. "Let's go," he said to me.

I started to follow him up the stairs when Dem called after us, letting us know he was tagging along. I left Nathan and Dem waiting for me in the foyer while I executed a quick change, then we piled into the SUV together. As we headed toward Plaka, I recognized the route.

"Is there a reason we are heading to the bar?" I asked.

"I need to talk to someone," Nathan answered.

Jen... "Why?" I asked.

He glowered, dodging the question, and parked the SUV in the alley behind the bar, which was packed, as usual. An alternative-rock band was on stage and this time of night, it was standing room only. We wove our way through the crowd and up to the bar. Jen was busy calming down a bachelorette party. One of the waitresses grabbed a bottle of whiskey, poured a glass, and handed it to Nathan. He leaned over and kissed her on the cheek, then watched as she sashayed over to get Jen's attention. I looked up at Dem, and he just rolled his eyes.

Finally, Jen was able to get away from the bride-to-be who was having too much whiskey.

"Hey, guys, didn't know you were coming in," Jen said.

"We're not staying," Nathan said to her.

"What can I do for you that Marcy hasn't already helped you with?" she said, winking at Nathan.

"Where's Ares, Jen?" Nathan asked.

Jen knows Ares?

"I haven't seen him. Not since the other night."

"He's one of your clients, and he attacked me and Lex last night, nearly killing her. Where is he?"

Holy shit. Nathan was holding back his anger. I wasn't sure how they knew each other, but I got the sense it had been personal at one point.

"He stays in one of the townhouses behind the bar from time to time," Jen answered, hurrying over to the highly intoxicated bridal party.

I looked over at Nathan. "What do we do now?"

"Pay him a house call," Nathan said.

I raised an eyebrow. "I had no idea there were houses behind the bar."

"Can't see what's there if you're not really looking," Dem said.

Truer words were never spoken. I'd come to Greece to find something, but what I've been looking for hasn't been easy to locate.

Nathan, Dem, and I left the bar and, as plain as day, fifteen yards behind the back entrance, sat a row of homes. Nathan walked up the stairs to the front door and twisted the doorknob, ripping it off the hinges. Something was wrong. The air was thick and sticky, like we'd just walked into a sauna.

"Do you smell that?" I asked no one in particular.

"Sulfur. Watch your back," Dem said.

It was eerily quiet—the only noise came from the clock in the foyer. We broke off to explore the rest of the house. I took the bedroom and found everything in disarray. The bed was broken in half, mirrors smashed, dressers overturned, and drawers thrown about. I reached the bathroom and smelled blood before I opened the door. When I walked in, I saw that every wall was covered in it.

Something caught my eye—the tub, the shower curtain flecked with blood. Bit by bit, I reached out and pulled the curtain back. Bile rose in my throat. I took a step back and covered my mouth with my hand, turned around to walk out, and slammed into a wall of muscle. I was about to stumble backward, but Nathan caught my shoulders and steadied me. Glad that his strong arms were holding me, I just shook my head.

It wasn't a body I'd seen, but body parts floating on top of bloody water. They'd belonged to a human female. Behind her ear was the same symbol I'd seen on the girl at the temple a few days ago.

Nathan's strong hands weighing on my shoulders calmed me. An electrical current raced through me and into Nathan. At first,

I wasn't sure if he'd noticed—it was so small—but when I looked into his eyes I saw that he had. We stood like that for a few moments, just taking in the new sensation that surrounded us. Something about him comforted me. His eyes had turned back to crimson. It was now my favorite color.

There was a time and place for everything, and now wasn't the time or the place to experiment with sentimentality. Dem cleared his throat, causing Nathan and I to jump apart like two negative charges.

He smiled down at me, a smile of unspoken pleasure. I watched as he turned and walked away, his graceful walk in stark contrast to his predatory nature. I investigated the adjoining room. Every sound echoed off the walls: the pushing aside of the shower curtain, the sound of water moving. There wasn't much evidence. I waited by the front door while they finished up.

"I can't tell how long she's been dead," Nathan said, and headed out the door.

"Where are we going?" I asked.

"To get a drink."

Somehow, the bar was even more packed than it had been when we left. I struggled to Jen, who was running around filling drinks like a bartending dervish. She saw me and walked right over.

"Hey Lex, what can I get you?"

"Whiskey and coke and two scotch on the rocks."

She raised her eyebrows and I laughed. "Not all for me."

She handed me the filled glasses and sighed.

"Did you find Ares?" she asked cautiously.

"No." I figured I'd leave it to Nathan and Dem to tell her the rest. She didn't ask any more questions and turned to help a customer who was trying to get her attention. I took the drinks and walked over to the booth, where Nathan and Dem were deep in a conversation that ended abruptly when they saw my face. Nathan held out his hand to grab the scotch from me.

"What's wrong?" he asked.

I sat down next to Nathan, trying not to get too close. "That girl had the same tattoo as the other one. What're you going to tell Jen?" I asked.

"The truth. I just want to know why Ares killed her. What's the motive and what, if anything, does this have to do with Zeus?" Nathan said.

I looked around the bar, noticing the other patrons. The female customers were gawking at Nathan and Dem, but they'd turn away when they caught me looking at them. One bold woman in a low-cut red dress—it showed off every curve and was cut to her mid-thigh—sauntered over. Her eyes were fixed on Nathan. Another woman from her group headed straight for Dem. Neither spared me a look. Red jutted a hip and pushed out her voluptuous chest.

"Hello, lover." Her tone was laced with sex.

"Good evening, Melanie," Nathan said unenthusiastically.

Melanie pushed out her lower lip in a pout. "Aren't you going to get up and give me a proper greeting? Or is this child in your way?" she asked, nodding at me.

I was about to stand up and throttle her, when Nathan seized my wrist under the table, holding me still.

"What do you want, Melanie?"

I watched her frustration rise and noted that Dem was having his own problems. Melanie's friend was trying to get him out on the dance floor. I let out the chuckle I'd been holding in and Melanie turned her eyes on me, looking like she would spit fire.

"What are you laughing at, bitch?" she snapped.

"Careful," was all I said to her.

Melanie looked pissed. She stormed off and called over her shoulder, "April!"

April looked at Melanie's retreating back, clearly not wanting to follow. I excused myself to the ladies' room, imagining two pairs of smoky eyes following me as I strode through the crowd. I was lucky—no one else was in the facility. But as I started washing my hands, someone came up behind me. Before she got a chance to smash my head into the sink, I ducked under her arm, twisted around, and grabbed her wrist with one hand and the back of her head with the other. I pinned her up against the wall with her back to me and held her tighter as she started to struggle.

"You thought I wouldn't notice you sneaking up on me?"

"Who the fuck are you?" Melanie screeched.

"Someone you don't want to fuck with. You try anything again, and I won't hesitate to snap your pretty neck."

For emphasis, I let my power roll off me and into her, pushing her body harder into the wall. I enjoyed the satisfying sound of crushing bone.

"All right! All right!" she squealed.

I let go of her and watched as she backed out of the bathroom while I returned to washing my hands. Some people never learn. When I emerged from the bathroom, I noticed Jen was conferring with the guys. Melanie was nowhere to be seen. Maybe she'd left, smart girl.

"You were gone a long time," Dem commented when I sat down.

"I ran into a friend."

"She left breathing, right?" Nathan asked with a smile.

I just shrugged.

A waitress had just come over to take our order when the man and woman I'd seen at the temple walked in. I grabbed Nathan's arm and looked up at the waitress.

"Give us a minute, please," I said. The waitress nodded and left. I pointed toward the bar where the man and woman took a seat. "Those are the people I told you about. The ones I overheard talking about the prophecy."

"So?" Nathan said.

"So? So maybe they can tell us what it means."

"Lex, they're humans. What would they know?"

"Why are you against talking to them?"

"We need to find Zeus to stop this prophecy from coming true. To do that, we need to talk to Hades. Those humans are not going to know any more than we do, so drop it."

I didn't understand what Nathan's hang-up was. These humans apparently had information about this prophecy, and he was not even willing to find out what it was. They could even help us find Zeus! It was almost like he didn't want to find him.

I didn't care what Nathan said. I stood up and walked up to them: Kevin and Darla. Nathan's eyes drilled holes into my back. I sat to the left of Darla and ordered another drink, then eavesdropped as they talked about the weather. I was about to give up —they weren't saying anything important—when Darla mentioned the prophecy.

"Excuse me," I interrupted. "I'm sorry to bother you, but I'm from the university and I'm doing a paper about myths and legends, and I couldn't help but overhear your conversation about a prophecy? I would really love to pick your brain, if that's all right…" I wasn't sure if they would agree. Kevin looked at me a little suspiciously, but Darla just smiled.

"Of course, dear. What are you studying?" she asked.

Shit. I had to come up with something fast or they wouldn't tell me anything.

"Archeology." Darla smiled and nodded her head.

"That's a wonderful profession."

Most of what she told me about the prophecy was old news, but when she mentioned it might allude to something else, my ears perked up.

"I do believe the prophecy is a little misleading," she said.

"What do you think it means?" I asked.

"The Kingdom of Light is, no doubt in my mind, referring to Zeus," Kevin began. "The second part mentions lying down with divine power bringing on eternal darkness. I believe it means a child of Zeus will bring about the second war."

"Zeus has a ton of kids. What's so special about this one?" I asked.

"We're not sure," Darla said with a sigh.

Damn. I looked back at Nathan and watched him follow a man out the back door. Something told me to follow. I excused myself and advanced through the crowd, keeping my eyes on Nathan's back. A guy wanting to buy me a drink waylaid me, but I kindly said no and kept walking. I opened the back door to the alley, following the voices.

"I want the truth, Akesios," Nathan growled.

I walked up beside Nathan. Akesios was beautiful. Tall like Nathan but built slightly smaller. His black hair was secured in a bun. It was his eyes that drew me, ice blue. He stared straight at me. So, this is Lucian's informant.

"Wow," he said. "You look just like her."

"Who?" I asked.

"Zeus's daughter."

Akesios looked over at Nathan, then back at me. "She died. A long time ago."

"Where can we find Zeus, Akesios?" Nathan snapped.

But Akesios wasn't paying attention to Nathan. He reached for me, but Nathan snatched his arm.

"Don't touch her," Nathan growled.

Akesios snapped back to attention. "I don't know where Zeus is. None of us do."

"Wait a minute. You're Akesios, you're Lucian's informant!"

"Who is Lucian?" Nathan asked.

I ignored his question.

Akesios looked at me. "Yes. Akesios is a name I use around humans. If you're going to address me, do it properly."

I looked back and forth between him and Nathan. "Okay, what do you want me to call you?" I asked.

"Apollo," he said simply.

"Do you know anything about the dead girl we found at Ares's place?" I asked.

"She was my charge."

Nathan and I exchanged a look.

"I didn't kill her."

"Why would Ares?" Nathan asked.

"First of all, he would because he's Ares. Secondly, I think it's a way to coerce the Gods into siding with him. The girl at Zeus's temple was a way to get you," he pointed at me, "so you'd think Zeus killed her and would take him out. There is a war starting, but Zeus isn't responsible. The girls are being used as incentive, I'm just not sure what kind yet."

"If Zeus has no part in this, then who does?" I asked.

"I am not the one who can tell you."

"Who is then?"

"Zeus."

I wanted to scream. "And why are *you* looking for him?"

"We need his help, and so do you. I'm afraid if the prophecy comes true, and this war starts again, it's not just humans who are fucked."

"Doesn't the prophecy relate to Zeus?" I asked.

"Yes, but it's misinterpreted."

"What do you think it means?"

Apollo didn't get to answer because right then, Dem walked out the back of the bar. "Jen wants to talk to you," he said to Nathan.

I turned back to Apollo, but he was gone. Ugh. I was getting tired of people—sorry, Gods and demons—being so cryptic. It was like everyone was too scared to talk to me, like I was some kind of delicate flower. It's annoying.

Jen was sitting in the booth with Dem, waiting for us. We'd barely sat down when the questions started coming. "How do you know it was one of my girls?" There was a hint of sorrow in her voice.

"I saw the tattoo, Jen," I said.

"Ares came in the other night. He's one of Jules's regulars and he seemed pretty pissed off, so I told Jules to stay away from him. Guess she didn't listen," Jen said.

"I'm still not understanding what this has to do with Zeus. If he is not a client, then the dead woman at the temple was a frame job and I'd like to know why," I said.

"So do I, but we can't find him at the moment," Nathan said.

I took a quick moment to fit all the puzzle pieces together. The dead woman at Zeus's temple is definitely connected to the woman at Ares's place because of the tattoo. I'm beginning to think the frame job is a way to get the Gods who are not willing to pick a side to cooperate. I think the girls are some sort of "payment" to get more players on Ares's team. I also want to know about the relationship between Apollo and Lucian. How did that happen? What other Gods could be in on this? The prophecy states that when the Kingdom of Light lies down with divine power, it will basically be the end of every-thing. The humans, Darla and Kevin, believe it has to do with a child of Zeus. Maybe that's the whole point of this. What if Zeus's kid is out there and Ares is trying to find it, and use it to start a war? Ares can clearly start a war on his own, so why would he need someone else to help him? If this kid is as powerful as everyone says, Ares could have a direct path to the throne.

It was getting late and we were all exhausted, so we headed to the car. Nathan pulled out his cell phone to call Raider and Dem opened the front passenger door for me and climbed in the back seat. The silence stretched between us and the SUV felt cruelly small.

"I know what you're thinking," Dem said.

"Oh yeah?" I asked. "How?"

"Because we've all thought the same thing: is all of this worth it?" Dem said.

It's hard to convince yourself there will never be consequences for your actions. Time was moving incredibly fast and sometimes it's hard to process events when the details are blurry.

"I'm not so sure," was all I said.

Maybe we had gotten all this wrong. What if Zeus had never returned? Why would Oberon send me to kill Zeus if he wasn't even in Greece? If I was chasing a ghost, then those two kids had died in vain by my hand. I would live with that for the rest of my life. What a way to spend eternity, huh?

I leaned my head back on the headrest, closed my eyes, and imagined the life I'd left behind in Avalon—days spent training, splashing my feet in the ocean, hanging out with Marius, Lana, and Jazzy...Oberon's obsessive need to make me his queen. Ugh. Of course, the grass isn't always greener on the other side.

The driver's side door opened, then slammed shut. I opened my eyes and glanced over at Nathan.

"Did you reach Raider?" I asked.

"Yeah, he's heading to Ares's place to do one last sweep."

"Sweep of what? Didn't you guys go through the place?" I asked.

Nathan looked at Dem in the rearview mirror.

"Raider can locate things we might have missed," Nathan said.

I looked at him suspiciously.

"How?" I asked.

"He just can," Nathan answered. He was hiding something. His back was hunched and his knuckles were turning white from gripping the steering wheel. He saw me looking at him and he calmed.

Fine, Mr. Secretive. Questions invaded my mind, although I doubted I'd get any answers. What could Raider do that Nathan or Dem couldn't? Why was he so special? I laughed to myself. Raider *was* special. I turned to look out the window and watch the world fly by. Greece was beautiful and I loved this city. It was hard to imagine the darkness that lay behind its beautiful canvas.

Zeus wants to destroy mankind and take over the world. Well, people in hell want water.

We pulled into the driveway of the castle and parked. Nathan got out first, followed by Dem, but I lingered a little longer. I watched as they retreated inside. I stepped out of the SUV and looked up to the sky: was what Hades said about Oberon really true?

Though the castle sat atop a mountain overlooking the ocean, it was nestled on thousands of acres of woods. I ventured a little farther into them, hiking to the cliff's edge to take in the sights. The moon was full, settled high in the clear dark night, its reflection glowing off the still water. I didn't pay much attention to the rustling behind me. Oops.

Something grabbed me from behind. I bucked forward, grabbing its arms to throw it off. It didn't work—whatever this was, held on for dear life. I threw myself back, hitting the ground, and heard a loud grunt. It let go for a quick moment and was able to roll out of the way and jump into a defensive stance. Holy shit.

8

---

*E*verything has its own scent, and some odors are more potent than others—like that of the thing that was lying in front of me. I tried not to gag, but it was difficult. It tried to get up and I kicked it in the face hard enough that whatever was left of its skull exploded under my boot. Something hit me from the side like a freight train; I looked up and saw massive teeth chomping at my neck. I struggled to keep it from turning my face into ground meat, clenching my teeth as it pushed against my arms. *Fuck*, I thought. *I need to work out more.* How the fuck did these things get here? The guys were clearly lacking in the surveillance department.

This thing had serious strength; I couldn't even muster enough energy to throw a bolt at it, let alone flash. A disgusting idea popped into my head. I freed one of my hands, grabbed at the thing's face and easily tore its flesh free. Blood and flesh sprayed all over me—some even got in my mouth. *Fucking gross.* Teeth kept coming after me.

"Fuck this."

I let the thing go and it fell forward and took a chunk out of my shoulder. I screamed. That. Fucking. Hurt. I swung my arm and punched it hard in the jaw, sending the mangled piece of my shoulder flying. I kicked the thing off and stood up, but two more creatures came running down the hill. Where the fuck were they coming from? Where the fuck were the guys?

As if they'd read my mind, Nathan flashed in, Dem close on his heels.

"About fucking time," I said, a little aggressively.

Nathan looked my way and I was taken aback. His face changed for a split second. At first it was Nathan I saw, then it was something else. If I hadn't been looking, I would have missed it. Something was behind those magnetic eyes.

He ran past me, barreling into the creature with the missing face. In one swift motion, Nathan ripped its head off. Dem walked over, holding the severed heads of the other two creatures.

"What took you guys so long?" I asked, exasperated.

"We had other pressing matters to deal with," Nathan said.

"I beg your pardon?" I said incredulously.

"Did I stutter?"

What the fuck was Nathan's problem? He turned and stalked off toward the castle. Dem came up and touched my arm.

"You good?" he asked.

I pulled away, gently—I didn't want to hurt Dem's feelings. "I'm fine."

I walked toward the house, Dem following behind. This thing with Nathan was *not* over. I entered the foyer, almost accidentally hitting Dem in the face with the door and stormed into the kitchen; Nathan was at the fridge grabbing a beer.

"Hey! What's wrong with you?" I snapped.

He turned around. "Nothing's wrong with me," he said, nonchalantly.

"Don't give me that bullshit. You made it perfectly clear I was taking you away from whatever it was you were doing."

"What I was doing was more important than you."

I grabbed a dining chair and threw it right at him. His attitude pissed me off. He was acting like it was my fault we had been attacked. Before the chair reached him, he flashed to me and pushed me up against the wall. The chair crashed into the cupboards behind him, taking out a few hanging pots above the island. Nathan pressed his arm against my neck, but I wouldn't back down. His eyes had turned black, his face changing—evil stared at me.

"I'd watch myself if I were you," he growled.

Dem took that moment to come into the kitchen. "Hey!" he shouted and grabbed Nathan by the back of his shirt to pull him off me.

"What's going on?" he snapped.

I didn't answer. I stared at Nathan, who was standing behind Dem—the demon was gone. Nathan stormed out of the kitchen, the door slamming hard against the wall.

"You might want to watch what you say around him," Dem said.

"*He's* being a dick and *I* have to watch what *I* say?" I asked, surprised. "You guys are fucked up, you know that?"

"No argument here."

I stormed out. The second I'd slammed the door behind me, I flashed. I ended up in the alley behind Jen's bar and strode in through the back door. It was two thirty in the morning and the place was still packed. I walked up to the bar and an older gentleman stood and offered me his seat. I sat down and silently nodded. Jen had help behind the bar, which was good because she needed it. She saw me and walked over.

"Hey love," she said cheerily. Then, she took in my appearance and her smile changed. "You look like shit," she said.

I laughed. She poured me a drink and a shot for herself. I rolled the drink around in my glass, focusing on the continued motion.

"Lex, what's up?" she asked.

"Just trying to figure out what the fuck I'm doing," I said, still staring at the bottom of my glass. It was all hitting me at once. The mission, the constant back and forth with Nathan.

"Everyone here is trying to figure out that exact thing," Jen said.

I smiled slightly. Someone familiar walked into the bar, but I didn't turn around to acknowledge him. He walked up and sat down on the stool next to me.

"Are you here to collect me?" I said.

"Nope. Just here for a drink," Raider said.

I stood to leave.

"Sit down."

I hesitated, then reclaimed my seat and we sat in silence. Raider called Jen over and when she saw Raider, I noticed a change in her. She stood up straighter, her smile was more endearing, and her eyes sparkled. Interesting.

"Scotch, and another for her," he said motioning to me. Raider smiled and winked at her. "Interesting night," he said.

"Who you telling?" I answered.

Raider laughed.

"It was like something out of a fucking horror movie," I shivered.

"They're hell-born demons—hell-demons. They have that effect on people."

I looked over at him.

"Violent, vile, power hungry…" he said.

"Why were they at the castle?" I asked.

"My guess? Hades sent them."

"How can you be so sure?"

He gave me a look that said, *Are you really that stupid?* "God of the Underworld, remember?"

"How'd they get on the grounds?" I asked.

"Not sure," he answered.

I sighed heavily while Raider considered me.

"Nathan would risk his life for any of us. Hell, he has. More than once…" Raider began.

I cut him off. "Why are you telling me this?" I asked.

"So you'll understand. It's not easy dealing with the side of yourself you can't control."

"Everyone has parts of themselves they don't like," I said.

"Not like his."

"Want to elaborate?"

"That's for him to tell."

"Did you find anything at Ares's place?" I asked.

"Now that you mention it…"

Raider handed me a gold ring with an aquamarine stone surrounded by pink diamonds. I took it and scrutinized it, recognizing it immediately. I always thought it was ugly, but why would it be at Ares's place? In that moment, my whole world began to fall apart.

"You recognize it don't you?" Raider asked.

I silently nodded. "It belongs to Oberon." Oberon was the other player Apollo mentioned.

Raider was silent for a moment. I was having a hard time processing everything. For the first time in my life, I felt completely lost. I looked around and noticed the bar was starting to clear out. The band was putting their instruments away and people were paying their tabs and filing out into the quiet night. The clock above the bar read three in the morning. Raider stood up.

"It's getting late," he said.

"I'll catch up with you later," I responded.

He looked down at me.

"You're coming back, right?"

"Would you miss me?" I laughed.

Raider just stared, clearly not amused. I nodded. Nathan and I hadn't gotten off on the right foot and I wasn't sure if we'd ever find our stride, we were too much alike. Volatile and stubborn—

we were in constant battle and neither of us was willing to fold. Raider hesitated, then headed out the door. I stood and proceeded to call it a night.

"Everything okay, love?" Jen asked when she walked over.

"Yeah, just need some sleep."

She looked at me with curiosity, like she had something on her mind. I was not in the mood to chat so I said goodbye and headed out the door. The streets of Plaka were quiet—the bars had closed and the streets were empty. I couldn't bring myself to go back to the castle, not tonight. There were too many things I needed to work out and being around Nathan was not going to help. He distracted me too much.

I headed to the bed-and-breakfast I'd stayed at when I first arrived. The bell on the door tinged above my head; I smiled. The receptionist was a young girl around twenty with red hair and freckles on her nose. Her smile was warm and cheery.

"Good evening. What can I do for you?" she asked.

"I would like a room for the night, please." I smiled precariously. I was exhausted, pissed, and on edge. The girl gave me the keys to a second-floor room where I promptly fell onto the bed and into a deep sleep.

I WOKE up the next morning in a sweat. My sleep had not been undisturbed; images of my parents' murder had run through my head all night and the soulless eyes of the two dead women stared at me. The sun was creeping through the shuttered window as I dressed in the same clothes I'd worn the night before, grabbed my black leather jacket, and headed downstairs. I'd search for Zeus myself. I needed to find the humans I'd seen at the bar, maybe they had some insight into this prophecy that could help me find Zeus. The girl at the front desk from last night was gone, replaced by a lady in her sixties. I smiled and proceeded to the front door.

"One moment dear," she called after me.

I turned around.

"A nice-looking young man dropped this off for you early this morning."

She held out a cell phone. I took it and frowned. There was a sticky note attached to it with a phone number and directions telling me how to turn on the fucking thing. Seriously? I dialed the number and Nathan answered on the first ring.

"Are you kidding me?" I began. "You don't think I know how to use a cell phone?"

"Come outside," was all he said before hanging up.

I thanked the receptionist and left, hopping into the black SUV I now saw had been parked right out front. Nathan didn't speak or apologize for last night;—it was an awkward drive. I leaned my head against the headrest and looked out the window, not even realizing we'd reached the castle till we drove up the driveway. Nathan parked and got out, and I followed a few moments later. When we were close to each other, I felt an electrical charge like I'd stuck my finger in a light socket.

I walked into the castle behind Nathan. It had been a long night and promised to be an even longer day. He didn't ask me about the ring Raider found at Ares's right away, I guessed he was waiting for me to say something. I followed him down to the cellar and through the hallway to the lonely door that loomed ahead of us—the same door behind which I'd interrogated Vic. When Nathan opened the door, a putrid smell hit my nose like a punch from a three-hundred-pound boxer.

A mutilated body is not the first thing you'd imagine seeing when you walk into someone's house. This was clearly not an ordinary house.

"Performing surgery?" I asked sarcastically.

Dem looked up at me, he was knee-deep in gore.

"I was looking for this."

He held up a small metal object the size of a matchbox. Wires ran from the bottom to the top with everything attached to a black button. I held my hand out and he placed it in my palm. I scrutinized it.

"What is it?" I asked

"A tracking device," he answered.

I looked up at Dem and Nathan. "How'd you know it was in that thing?" I asked, pointing to the body on the table.

"When Nathan ripped its head off, he found it embedded in its neck."

"Where is it tracking from?" I asked.

"Romania," Nathan said.

I looked up at him, surprised.

"How the fuck did the creature get here? What was it doing here? Why?" I asked.

"We're still trying to figure that out," Nathan said.

I handed the device back to Dem and he placed it carefully on the table next to the body.

"What now?" I asked.

"The logical move would be to go to Romania and try to backtrack the signal," Dem said. He saw the look on my face and laughed. "Of course, that is out of the question."

"We need to talk to Hades. I bet he sent those things, and we could ask him about Zeus," I said.

"Hades isn't that stupid. He'll smell a trap the second we're at his door," Nathan said.

"You've got a better idea?" I asked, and walked up the stairs out of the cellar. I went to the kitchen, I needed to get my energy up. I opened the fridge and grabbed a bottle of wine, popped the top, and drank straight from the bottle. No shame. Someone cleared their throat. It was Dem, leaning against the door, arms crossed over his chest, giving me an amused look. I wiped my mouth on the back of my hand.

"What?" I asked.

Dem just laughed and shook his head. He walked toward me, grabbed two glasses out of the cupboard behind me, took the bottle from my hand, and poured us both a drink.

"Grabbing a drink before your rendezvous with Hades?" Dem chuckled.

I drank the rest of the wine in my glass, then snatched the bottle he'd put on the counter.

"It's not a rendezvous."

Dem put his hands up in surrender. "No one is stopping you from talking to Hades. I just want to make sure you understand the consequences if you do."

"Believe me, I understand," I said honestly.

I made for the door, but Dem stopped me; the look he gave me was confusing.

"We're not against you, you know," Dem said.

"Maybe not you."

I left it at that and walked out. I headed toward the front door, pulling myself together, then stopped short—I had no way to get to him. A silver Shelby Mustang GT500 pulled up and Nathan rolled down the window.

"Get in."

"Where're we going?" I asked.

He gave me a look that said, *Get in the fucking car,* so I slid into the passenger seat. I swear the car got smaller with each passing minute, the awkwardness between Nathan and I was making me claustrophobic. We drove into the country, rolling hills on one side, expansive, clear blue waters on the other. This was my idea of what the humans call "paradise." Avalon is beautiful, but compared to this?

"What changed your mind?" I asked Nathan.

"I haven't changed my mind," he said.

"Then what are you doing here?" I asked.

"I figured you'd do something stupid and get yourself killed."

"You know, if you're going to be a dick, you can just pull over and let me out," I said angrily.

Nathan laughed. I'd never heard the sound before, so it was a little odd. It was a deep, rich sound that made me smile despite the fact that I was frustrated with him. His expressionless look was back in place a second later. I laid my head back on the head-rest—this promised to be a fun ride. After another forty minutes of silence, Nathan pulled onto a dirt road. I sat up a little straighter and noticed the gorgeous two-story Greek-style home that loomed in front of us. Nathan clocked the expression of awe on my face.

"If you knew where Hades lived, why insist on meeting him at the club? Why even have informants?" I asked.

"Hades never really stays put for too long, so there's no guarantee he'd be anywhere. The club was easy because he's there rather frequently. If I can't track him down, I have people who can. Also, he reached out to us."

"So there's no way to know if he's home." It was a statement.

Nathan just shrugged. "If he is, there is no way to know what his reaction will be," he said.

"Hades won't kill me."

"What makes you think that?"

"I have something he wants."

"And that is?"

I gave myself the once-over, insinuating that all Hades was after was my body.

We parked in front of the house and I got out of the car deliberately, expecting a trap. I wouldn't put anything past Hades. The place was eerily quiet. Nathan stepped out of the car just as cautiously; we could trip an alarm with any move.

"What's your plan?" Nathan asked.

"Ring the doorbell, of course."

Nathan raised an eyebrow but I just shrugged in response. If there were cameras, he already knew we were here, so why bother sneaking around? We avoided the front door and headed around to the back of the house. The backyard was immaculate; large apple trees, plum trees, and a water fountain took up most of the manicured lawn. I walked up to the back door with Nathan right behind me. All of a sudden, the floor underneath me shook. Nathan held me.

"You've gotta be fucking…"

That's all I said before Nathan and I fell through the trapdoor. I hit the ground hard after falling for what felt like forever, or close to it. As I rolled over onto my stomach, my bones cracked and popped. Fuck. When I was able to get my bearings, I looked around. We were in a concrete basement. Dried blood was splattered all over the walls and floor. Meat hooks hung from the ceiling five feet from where we landed. A few more feet and I'd have been hanging by my bottom lip. I pushed myself up, looking around for Nathan. He was already looking for a way out. *Thanks for helping me up, buddy,* I growled in my head. I figured we'd be here awhile, so I took a seat on a metal chair and watched Nathan pace back and forth, anger and frustration radiating off him.

For hours, Nathan slammed his fist against the concrete wall, trying to break it down. I didn't understand what he wasn't getting; the wall obviously wasn't going to budge. He was livid that he'd decided to come and of course, he blamed me entirely. One last fist slam and he split his knuckles.

"Feel better?" I asked sarcastically.

Nathan glared at me, but I just shrugged my shoulders.

"Being pissed at me is not going to help," I said.

"Maybe if you had just listened, we wouldn't be in this mess again," Nathan said.

"Hey, I didn't ask you to come or drag you here, so don't blame this on me."

He knew I was right, even if he'd never admit it. He took a deep breath.

"Okay, ole wise one, what's your suggestion for getting out of here?" he mocked.

"Don't be a dick," I shot back.

"Figure out what the fuck you're doing, and I won't."

"Fuck you, Nathan."

This was getting us nowhere. We were both too stubborn.

"What's your problem?" I asked him.

He turned to me and I was taken aback by the look in his eyes.r

"My *problem* is your knack for going off half-cocked, getting into situations that you can't control, and asking me and us to trust you."

"Neither you nor Dem came up with a better idea. You all but left me on that hill to get my face chewed off and you acted like it was my fault," I snapped.

"You need to fucking pay attention to what's going on around you. Don't get yourself fucked then ask me to trust you on blind faith."

"What do you want from me, Nathan? Do you want me to apologize for being myself? I'm not used to doing things any other way. It might not be what you want or how you like things done, but maybe seeing a situation from a different perspective can solve the problem."

I ticked off everything that had gone wrong since I started this mission. I had two deaths on my conscience; a God trying to fuck me, kill me, or both; three demons who want me to disappear in some fashion; and another God who's gone MIA. I had almost started to forget why I was in Greece in the first place and I was no closer to figuring out how to navigate this whole fucking mess.

"Giving up, huh?" Nathan said.

"I'm not giving up, I'm contemplating."

He raised an eyebrow. "Contemplating what exactly?" he asked

"How to save your ass."

He laughed, throwing his head back. "Ha. That's fucking rich."

"What I think is rich is that you don't trust me to get us out of this," I said.

"Well, to be honest, you haven't been useful so far."

"One of these days you're going to realize you can't piss without me," I said.

"If that day ever happens, I'll make sure I never have to piss again."

We sat in silence. *Aren't we a ray of sunshine?* I thought. The world was starting to feel a little too small for the both of us. His magnetic persona was taking up the little space we were occupying; it rubbed against me, and not in a good way. His irritation was oppressive.

"Would you ever have thought that this is where your life would end up?" I asked.

"What?" he asked.

I looked over at him.

"Trying to save a species that doesn't even know that things like us exist?"

Nathan sighed. "I never thought I'd meet someone so hell-bent on trying to prove something to herself while fulfilling the needs of others."

"It's my job," I replied.

"Ditto. However, I imagine you had a choice."

"I want the truth," I said.

"Truth about what?"

"Everything," I answered.

He raised an eyebrow.

I dug in my pocket and pulled out the ring Raider found at Ares's and handed it to Nathan.

"Raider found it at Ares's place. It belongs to Oberon, which makes me think Hades might be right. Of course, Hades could be lying, but what if it's true? What if Oberon did kill my parents, and he's working with Ares? What if this whole thing was a setup for me to kill Zeus so Oberon could claim the throne?"

"Where does Ares fit into this scenario? Ares is likely after the throne himself."

"I don't know." I was quiet for a moment. "Oberon proposed before I left."

"Ah. What was your answer?" he asked.

"I didn't give him one. He wants my answer when all this is over."

"What do you want?" he asked.

"I don't want that life," I said honestly.

"That doesn't answer the question."

I paused. "To be free."

It was bare-bones honesty. It was all I'd ever wanted. My life had been protected from the day I was born. I was treated differently, like I was fragile. Don't get me wrong, doing what I do is pretty kick-ass but I'm always at the mercy of someone else. I always followed someone else's rules, never mine. Oberon knew I didn't love him, but it had never stopped him from hoping that one day I would. That day would never come.

"So, what are you going to do?" Nathan asked.

I looked over at him. "I don't know."

"Maybe you could start by thinking up a way out of here," he smiled.

I scrubbed my hands down my face. *It's about time I stopped fucking up.*

"You don't always fuck up," Nathan said.

I looked over at him. "You read minds, too?"

"As I've said, your eyes give away everything."

"Should I keep my eyes closed?" I teased.

"You should stop thinking so much. Sometimes you just have to feel it."

"Life motto?" I joked.

"Friendly advice. Take what you want from it," he said flatly.

And we're back to being pissed off. I needed a drink. It's funny, because I never used to drink so much. Maybe it was the company. I stood up and examined the wall.

"Well, I can't flash us out of here, the wall's too thick."

"Yeah, figured that one out a while ago," Nathan grumbled.

I just ignored him. Suddenly, I saw the wall billow for a split second. What the fuck? I touched my palm to the thick concrete, and it rippled around me. Something grabbed my arm and tried to pull me in. I jerked back, stumbling into Nathan. We stole forward, and it rippled. As clear as day, I saw the castle.

"Fuck," Nathan said.

"I think this is how those things that attacked us at the castle got in," I said. I looked over at him. *I guess ladies first, huh?* I stepped up to the portal, but Nathan stopped me.

"You're not going through there."

"You got a better idea?"

He pushed me out of the way. *Oh no you didn't.* He walked up to the portal and stepped inside, violently it pushed him back. I chuckled, but he glared.

"Guess it doesn't like you," I mocked.

"All right, you try then."

I hesitated, then stepped up and started walking through. I looked back—Nathan's eyes were as wide as saucers. I grabbed his shirt collar and pulled him in with me.

9

*I*t was like walking through water, with the slightest resistance pushing against me. The closer we got to the castle, the farther away it looked and in a matter of seconds we were thrown out of the portal. I landed hard on the ground and Nathan thudded right next to me.

I pushed myself off the ground and looked up, expecting to see the castle. I was wrong. We weren't even in Greece anymore. We stood in a beautiful rainforest. The humidity was stifling... sort of like Nathan's mood. The trees sparkled in the brilliant sunlight. Flowers of every imaginable color grew in every different direction. Birds sang to each other. I was admiring everything around me when Nathan pulled me through another portal. This one was not so nice. It was desolate, dark, and the smell of sulfur singed my nostrils.

"We could've stayed in the other one a little longer," I said.

"I think that was its intention," Nathan replied.

"Why didn't we end up at the castle?" I asked.

"Portals can be very fickle," Nathan said.

"Why would Hades have a portal in his basement?" I asked.

"Beats me," Nathan answered.

Portals in Avalon were rare, too much risk of outside interference. We tried to limit how much exposure we got, so I never realized how many different worlds there were—I'd been pretty sheltered. After my parents were murdered, Oberon never let me venture too far.

Little did he know, I would venture far beyond his limited sight. I'd seen things most people can only imagine. I'd seen dark places and light, I'd seen places I'd never want to see again, and places I wanted to get lost in. Avalon was beautiful, but I wasn't so sure if it was the place for me anymore. Even in the darkest times, Avalon never brought me a sense of comfort; I never truly belonged. Maybe this new sense of freedom was getting to me. Whatever it was, I never wanted to lose it. But life is never one-dimensional and soon I would figure that out, whether I wanted to or not.

We walked in silence, trying to locate another portal that would get us to the castle before we got stuck, or worse. I had no sense of time. Did it move faster here than it did back in Greece? How far off the grid were we? It seemed the sun never set—it hung immobile in the dry air. I was getting agitated and annoyed that we weren't making any headway and Nathan wasn't too happy either. If we didn't find a portal soon, Nathan would have to carry me.

As if by some miracle, a portal appeared. Nathan stopped so quickly I ran right into him. The portal opened to the castle again. Nathan stepped toward it. I grabbed his arm and he looked back at me.

"How can you be sure it won't dump us somewhere else?" I asked.

"There's only one way to find out. You want to stay in here forever?"

Valid point. "After you," I said with a smile.

Nathan walked toward the opening with me close behind. He stepped through without incident, but I wasn't so lucky—it threw me back. I ran up to grab Nathan's hand, but the portal closed on me.

"Fuck!" I yelled.

How many times was I going to get shit on? I looked around frantically for another portal. Obviously they weren't popping up like daisies. I was determined to keep going. I needed to get back to Plaka and finish the mission.

I stopped walking. What had this mission gotten me anyway? Bruises and a bunch of shitty-behaved men who can't stand me. I turned and walked back the way I came. Fuck all this. Fuck the mission, fuck Oberon. I'd never wanted to be his queen, and that's exactly where I'd end up if I found Zeus, killed him, and returned to Avalon.

I was back where I started when I stopped again. Nathan. He's been a jerk, but there was something so *compelling* about him. I *knew* him. I'd forgotten for a minute about the Spyder Cell Marius gave me. Maybe he could help—I'm not sure how, but it was worth a try. I touched the cell on my neck, but nothing happened. I tried a few more times before I decided it was a waste. This damn thing is supposed to work everywhere, it's fucking magic!

The sun was hot; I was tired, pissed off, and in need of an energy boost, fast. A portal popped into the sky twenty feet ahead and instead of a hot wasteland—which I was currently in—it opened to an oasis. I walked up, half expecting it to throw me back, but to my surprise, I passed through easily. That was weird. Why did I have so much trouble with the other one?

The sky was dreadfully dark; the only light came from the moon reflecting off the water. The sand was light blue with specks of black. The air was fresh, and I took a deep breath, pleased it didn't singe my lungs. I wouldn't mind being stuck here. I loved the water. There's something about calm water that makes you stop and understand that all the shit that is going on in your life can be washed away by just a taste of oblivion.

I sat there watching the water crawl onto the sand and I understood why oblivion was so treasured. I wanted to get lost, to stop worrying about what was ahead of me and how I would deal with the truth. Maybe when all of this was over, I'd find my way back and experience my own oblivion. Hell, I'd already dared Nathan to take a shot. I sighed and got up. I looked around one last time before focusing on the task at hand. This place was beautiful.

After hours sitting at the edge of the water, I noticed the moon never left the sky, just like the sun had never set in the other place. The wind never picked up; there wasn't even a slight breeze. It was like the world had stopped, and the only thing that kept moving was me. There were no stars, so there was no way to tell if I was going the right way or not. Maybe I'd get lucky and a portal would just open in front of me. I waited. Nothing. But the energy in this place was helping me stay awake. I was beginning to feel that oblivion. The longer I was stuck in the portal, the more I worried I would waste away, that I would be forgotten.

But that wasn't what I wanted. I wanted to be part of something, part of a family. I wanted to be given a reason to leave my old life behind and explore the world, but I was realizing that it was a hard road to be on. I wanted Nathan to trust me, to see me as more than a "throw caution to the wind" type.

Everything around me looked the same even though I was pretty sure I'd been walking for miles. My eyes grew heavy. There wasn't anything to do but keep walking, but first, I needed some rest. I looked for cover, in case some flesh-eating thing came chomping at me again. Vibrant cypress trees sat back from the shore. I walked into the middle of a cluster, sat down, and leaned back against a massive tree trunk. In a matter of moments, my eyes closed.

I slipped into a dreamless sleep—my mind was too awake for dreams. I wasn't sure how long I slept, but at some point, my eyes flew open and I found myself strangely...immobile. I looked down and noticed I'd been tied to the tree I was leaning against. The rope was made of reinforced metal and spikes dug into my skin when I tried to move. *Just fucking great.*

A rustling sound came from the trees. My head jerked up and locked onto the empty eyes of...a child? She had shoulder-length curly blond hair and a beautiful face with sparkling amber eyes. Familiarity sat in my stomach; her presence caused fear and longing. She moved slowly, reaching her hands down to grab the metal rope.

"Don't!" I yelled.

I didn't want her to harm herself by touching the spikes on the rope. She stopped and looked up at me, staring at me for a few moments. It was the most curious feeling: warmth, sadness, acknowledgement, love—all those emotions shined through her eyes. She touched the metal rope and it fell to pieces. I watched as it sank into the ground.

I stood up and looked down at the little girl. I wanted so much to pick her up, hold her, and take her with me, but something told me this place was where she belonged. Loud noises came from behind me in the clearing. I looked around the tree and watched as a handful of vicious dogs, I'd later know to be hellhounds, barreled toward us. I turned to grab the girl and noticed she wasn't behind me anymore. I turned back; she was standing in the clearing waiting for the dogs to reach her. She was using herself as bait.

I lunged toward her, but a large gust of wind hit me from behind. A portal was opening, and I saw the castle in the distance. I'd bring the girl. I started to run for her, but something grabbed my arm, hard. I turned to see Nathan, who was pulling me into the portal. I struggled and watched in horror as the dogs descended on the child.

"No!" I screamed as she turned to me and smiled.

Nathan pulled me through as I struggled to get free. The last thing I saw before the portal closed was a dog the size of a horse pouncing on top of her. I stood staring into empty space. Nathan showed up, but I just looked right through him. I was relieved to see him, but I was also angry. He shook my shoulders and said my name, trying to get my attention. I shook myself into reality and instantly jumped at him.

"Why did you do that?" I snapped. "I could have saved her."

He looked at me oddly.

"Saved who? And you're welcome for saving your life," he growled.

"The little girl. She was right in front of me."

"Lex, I have no idea what you're talking about. There was no little girl."

"She was right there. She untied me and put herself between me and the dogs."

I was babbling, but I wasn't making this up.

"Okay. What did she look like?" Nathan asked patiently.

"She had curly blond hair, bright amber eyes. She had the most beautiful face I've ever seen. She was familiar, like I know her from somewhere."

I looked up at Nathan and all the beautiful light-golden color drained from his face.

"You all right?" I asked.

His demeanor changed back instantly.

"Fine."

With that, Nathan turned and headed toward the castle. I hesitated. What the hell was that about? Little did I know that this moment would become a major turning point in our relationship.

I noticed that the SUV was gone as I walked into the castle and beelined to the kitchen. Nathan was pouring himself a shot of whiskey and offered me one. *The day I've had,* I thought, sitting at the island, *I might just take two.* It was so quiet with no one else around; I'd begun to think of the castle as home and I'd missed

Nathan when I was stuck in the portal. Sitting in Hades' basement had given us time to just talk.

"Where're Raider and Dem?" I asked.

Nathan handed me the drink and stood on the other side of the island.

"Dem's in Romania, Raider's in the city," he said nonchalantly.

I choked on my drink.

"What?" I gasped.

"The tracking device emitted signals from Romania and here in Athens," he said.

"I just figured the signal had been hijacked to make it look like it was coming from Romania," I said.

"I thought that too, till Raider found a signal coming from Athens. So we decided to take a gamble," Nathan said.

"Wait, when did Raider find the other signal?" I asked.

"When I got out of the portal," he said.

"How long were we in there before you got out?" I asked.

"A week," he answered.

I was nervous to ask the next question; he'd gotten out before me, after all.

"How long was I in there?"

Nathan was quiet. He put his hands in his pockets and leaned into his heels. Was he afraid to tell me? Was he afraid of my reaction? He was having trouble looking at me.

"A month."

I spit out my drink. I was in that portal for an entire month? Did they even try looking for me? Or was it easier for them with me out of the way? Like Nathan said, I have a knack for fucking things up.

"I looked for you at Hades's house."

I sighed. I wanted to know if Hades was behind the attack on the hill, and why. I wanted to ask Nathan about the little girl I'd seen. I was totally confused, but I was certain he recognized her. I didn't ask.

"How long have Raider and Dem been gone?" I asked.

"They left a few days ago. I heard from Dem; he should be back tonight. Raider's staying in the city for a few more days and should be back by the end of the week."

That meant Nathan and I would be alone for the next few hours. *Just wonderful,* I laughed to myself.

"What happened in there?" Nathan asked.

"After the portal closed, I just started walking. I have no idea how long it was before the other portal opened. In that world, it was always night and I could see the ocean for miles. It was peaceful."

I paused a moment before continuing, "I didn't imagine that girl. I don't know what happened, but I fell asleep and when I woke up, I couldn't move. She looked at me like she knew who I was. It was funny, but I felt like I knew her, too. She saved my life."

Nathan kept quiet, relaxed. He wasn't betraying anything.

"When I told you what she looked like, you went completely still."

The front door slammed shut and Dem came into the kitchen dressed for a snowstorm. Perfect timing. He took off his winter coat and dropped it on the kitchen floor. Nathan looked over at Dem and cleared his throat, motioning to the coat which was producing a puddle of water on the floor. Dem just shrugged.

"Glad you're back," Dem said to me.

"Thanks."

"What'd you find?" Nathan asked.

Back to business as usual. Sometimes, I just wanted to take a break.

"A whole lot of fucking snow."

I smiled. Leave it to Dem to find humor in any situation. Nathan didn't look the least bit amused, just stood cold-faced with his arms across his chest. Dem took a seat next to me and motioned to Nathan to pour him a drink.

"Raider still in the city?" Dem asked.

Nathan nodded.

"Romania was a bust. As soon as I got close enough to the signal it shifted to another location," Dem explained.

"Where?" I asked.

Dem took a drink then looked at me.

"Here."

I looked up at Nathan. "In Athens?" I asked Dem. "How is that possible?"

"Those things were never in Romania. The tracking device emitted a false signal," Dem answered.

"Why?" Nathan questioned.

"My opinion? To send us on a wild goose chase. Whoever sent those things thinks we're getting too close to find Zeus."

"It must have been Hades. We found a portal in his basement that led directly to the castle," I said.

"Yes, but you weren't sent to the castle. Having a portal in your house doesn't mean you have a horde of demons shacking up in your basement."

"What do you think, then?" I asked Dem.

"I don't know yet."

I took the bottle of whiskey from Nathan and poured myself another drink. If Hades was planning something big, we'd wouldn't find out until it was too late. We were ultimately fucked.

"Now what?" I asked.

Dem poured himself another drink.

"Sleep. It's almost three in the morning," Dem said.

He stood, took the shot of whiskey, and turned to leave the kitchen.

"Goodnight Dem," I said to his back.

He turned back, smiled down at me, and kissed me on the cheek. Jealousy hit me like a ton of bricks—it was coming from Nathan, even though he appeared completely unaffected by the whole situation. Did I really feel his emotions or was it my wishful thinking? Apparently, Dem picked up on it too, because he just chuckled at Nathan and left. It was awkward, being alone with Nathan, but I was done playing games. I could enjoy the rest of the bottle upstairs in my room.

"Lex," Nathan said quietly, so quietly I almost missed it.

I stopped and turned around but he just stared at me. I turned back and continued up the stairs. I figured I deserved it after a month in the portal. A whole month and nothing had changed. Nathan still treated me like an enemy, and I was starting to forget why I was here.

The little girl. She invaded my subconscious at every moment. The look in her eyes would be embedded in my brain for as long as I live.

I would let it go with Nathan. He had his reasons for keeping quiet about the girl and I wouldn't push him. I needed to call Marius, hopefully it wasn't too late or too early.

"Your timing is terrible," Marius said when he answered my call.

"Did Oberon kill my parents?" I asked. Marius was quiet. "Marius, please tell me the truth."

I walked out onto the balcony, the night was beautiful and still.

"Lex, there are things I cannot answer for you."

"Tell me!" I yelled.

"Yes," he answered, with sorrow.

"Why?"

He sighed. "I don't know."

"This is all fucked up, Marius. What am I even doing here if Zeus wasn't responsible for my parents' death? Is this mission even legit? Is Avalon even in danger? What else aren't you telling me?"

There was silence on the other end. He was trying to protect me, but I didn't need to be protected; I needed the truth.

"How can I trust you if you won't be honest with me? By the way, I got stuck in a fucking portal for a month and the damn cell you gave me wouldn't even fucking work!" I hung up without anything more and climbed into bed, exhausted and hurt, longing for sleep. I closed my eyes as tears trickled down my cheeks.

I woke from the first full night of sleep I'd had since coming to Greece. I didn't dream of the little girl and part of me was glad but also a little disappointed. I wanted to know more, although I figured soon enough, I would learn more than I ever wanted to know. I didn't spare a thought for Marius, either. He was family and, as they say, those you love the most can hurt you the worst.

The smell of coffee hit me before I made it to the kitchen. When I walked in, I saw Nathan pouring a cup while Dem and Raider sat at the table along with Jen. That was interesting—she was everywhere lately. Maybe she'd stayed the night?

Nathan handed me the cup he'd just poured. Was that a smile?

"Thanks," I said.

He just nodded. I mentally rolled my eyes and took a seat next to Dem at the island. Everyone was quiet and Jen took that as her cue to leave. She said her goodbyes and headed out, then it was back to business.

"How was your trip to the other side?" Raider asked.

"Huh?" I asked, confused.

"Wherever it was you were for a month," Raider clarified.

"Enlightening."

"Did you find anything?"

I glanced at Nathan, then turned back to Raider and shook my head. Raider arched an eyebrow, then shrugged.

"Sounds like you had the same luck we did," Dem interjected.

"If what Apollo said is right, and Zeus isn't trying to resurrect some thousand-year-old war, why are we still looking for him?" I asked no one in particular.

"The prophecy," Nathan said.

"What about it? Earlier, you didn't even want to listen to me even though I might have valuable information."

"Alright, I'm listening."

"Those humans I talked to said the prophecy is about a child, Zeus's child."

Dem, Nathan, and Raider went completely still.

"What's wrong?" I asked.

Nathan shook his head. "Could be right, but they are just humans. Probably a bunch of conspiracy theories."

Ugg! I mentally shouted.

"I've been wondering something," Nathan said, changing the subject. "How was I able to make it through the second portal, but you weren't?"

"Good question. I have no idea."

"Things are starting to get complicated," Nathan said.

"You're just figuring that out now?" I asked jokingly.

"Lex is right, Hades will turn up eventually. Regardless of your apprehension toward these humans Nathan, there is a possibility they could be right," Dem said.

Dem's statement did not make Nathen look happy. Why was this such a big deal to him?

I replayed in my head what the hell we were doing. The guys wanted to find Zeus because of the prophecy claiming he will bring about total annihilation of mankind; a second war. Hades claimed to know where Zeus was, but because I refused his offer to be with him, he got pissed off and now he's MIA. Apollo said the dead prostitutes were some kind of incentive but he wasn't sure what for.

"Dem—you, me, and Lex will head to Zeus's temple, maybe we can find something there. Raider, I want you to stay here and revisit the site where the first portal opened up," Nathan ordered.

"What do you think we'll find at Zeus's temple?" I asked.

"I don't know, but I want to check it out anyway."

I pushed my chair out from under the island. At least I

wouldn't be alone with Nathan. Ever since I'd mentioned the little girl from the portal, he'd been more distant than usual. We piled into the SUV and headed to the temple.

It was midday, and it was getting warmer by the hour. On the positive side, the grounds around the temple were empty. If I walked into the temple and called for Zeus, would he appear? I laughed to myself and shook my head. *Like that would ever happen.* I couldn't wave a magic wand and make all my problems go away; this was a waste of time. We were going in circles and it was making me dizzy.

I walked into the temple to try my luck, just in case. Just looking at Zeus's sculpture unnerved me—I saw the power behind those eyes. An image formed in my mind: Zeus and Oberon standing next to a familiar young woman, though her face was obscured. The image faded. Why was this so hard to figure out? I was waiting for some miracle to drop in my lap and lead us to Zeus.

Wishful thinking, apparently. I met Nathan and Dem back at the car and climbed into the passenger seat while Dem slid into the seat behind me. Nathan's phone rang and he stayed outside while I closed the door. I watched Nathan walk in a circle, clearly engaged in the conversation with the person on the other end of the phone.

"He cares about you, you know," Dem said.

I was startled. I turned around and looked at Dem.

"What? That's rich," I laughed. "We've threatened each other and tried to kill each other. Not really a confession of love." Still though, I wasn't sure about Nathan. Was I hoping Dem was right? Maybe I was.

"He's not the romantic type, as you can tell," Dem answered back.

I saw Nathan heading back to the car.

"Just drop it, he's coming back," I said.

Dem snorted. "I think you like him, too."

"Shut up!"

Nathan climbed in behind the wheel and looked at both of us. I stared straight out the window but imagined Dem was sitting in the back seat with a big smile on his face.

"What's up, you two?" Nathan asked.

Did I have feelings for Nathan? I glanced at him out of the corner of my eye. He was drop-dead gorgeous, with a carnality about him that was almost frightening. His crimson eyes stared straight ahead but his breath caught—maybe he noticed I was checking him out. I retreated into my thoughts. We constantly argued, but there was an undeniable pull whenever we were together. I hated to admit to that judgment-clouding chemistry.

We drove the now-familiar road back to the castle in silence. The cafés were busy with patrons who were sitting outside enjoying the amazing summer weather—laughter and music floated on the air. It didn't hit me until we got in the car, but my energy was slowly draining. Being at Zeus's temple had caused my body to go into hyperdrive, like I'd received a supercharged energy boost. When we left, I was running on empty.

After we drove through the castle gate, Nathan parked the SUV. I took off my boots and when my bare feet touched the earth, everything rushed back into me. Nathan watched.

"What's it like?" he asked.

I held out my hand and he walked over. The moment he touched my fingers, that cold place grabbed onto him and a powerful charge ran through me and straight into him. He didn't flinch or try to break away. He rode the charge with me; it was intoxicating.

A very intimate vision of Nathan and I in bed ran through my mind. He was lying on top of me, our bodies warm and slick with sweat. His hand reached up and lightly brushed my hair off my face. His eyes were intense; I could see through to his soul. He wanted me to see him, see what he was. His thumb touched my cheek then caressed my lips before he kissed me deeply. The vision didn't feel the same as the one Hades had planted; It was more personal—it felt right. Was it his subconscious or mine? When it got too intense, I broke the charge.

We were both breathing hard and the look in his eyes was absolutely predatory. I backed away and darted toward the castle. He didn't follow, thank the Gods, but what just happened? I shook the thought from my head. I was afraid we'd both get hurt if we got too close.

I tore through my room, leaving a trail of clothes from the door to the bathroom. I've been distracted lately. I looked in the mirror—what a mess. I longed for bed, but just before I climbed in, I realized something didn't feel right, like someone was in the room. I looked around…nothing. The balcony doors swung open and I walked over and shut them. That cold place inside me went on full alert. Something flickered; Hades flashed in.

"What the…" I started.

Hades tried to grab me but I dodged him and kicked him back. He fell hard on the ground. I couldn't flash.

"You can't flash through the barrier."

"What do you want?" I snarled.

"You killed Vic. I'm impressed," Hades said.

"He made it easy. What do you want?" I snapped.

I heard banging on the door.

"You took Vic from me, now I'm going to take something from Nathan," Hades said.

Nathan, Raider, and Dem crashed through the door. Hades grabbed me, and we flashed. Fuck, I was screwed. The force was so strong, I lost consciousness.

a hard smack forced my eyes open. I was hit with so much power that it split my lip. Everything around me was blurry, as if oil covered the walls. Then, the realization came like an avalanche: I was in the center of a small room with my wrists tied tightly to a wooden chair. Hades stood before me, reeling with anger. It didn't show on his face but through how calm he was.

"I don't like hurting people," Hades started.

I raised an eyebrow.

He smiled. "Not really. Sometimes it's a necessity to get what you want. You should know that."

Yes, I did. "What do you want, Hades?"

"I want what I've wanted from the start. But right now, I feel like savoring this moment."

He touched my cheek, then leaned in for a kiss. I ducked just in time and he pecked my cheek. He chuckled.

"One day, you'll learn to enjoy my company."

"I highly doubt that," I answered.

He hit me again, this time with a closed fist. "Stupid bitch!"

He grabbed a six-inch blade from the metal table on my right and jabbed it into my leg. I screamed. Then, he took a hammer and slammed it down on my feet.

"I could put a stop to this," he said silkily.

Poison dripped from his words. I took a deep breath, trying to speak through the pain. "How about you explain why there's a portal in the basement of your house."

Hades regarded me for a moment. "I'm not accustomed to walking around like a human—it's easier with portals. Besides, I like to explore."

"That doesn't explain how it ended up behind the castle," I snapped.

"Portals are fickle," he said.

Where had I heard that before? Nathan. "I nearly got my face chewed off by a hell demon that came out of the portal. Want to explain that?" I demanded.

"I don't know what you're talking about."

"Liar. Demons are running rampant and the God of the Underworld has no idea?"

"Believe what you want, Lex. Now, tell me about Vic."

"He's dead."

"You killed him. I want to know why."

"Would you believe me if I said it was an accident?" I said innocently.

Hades looked at me with no amusement.

"He tried to kill me and it backfired and killed him instead. You said you had information on Zeus but you refused to tell us unless I gave myself to you, so we improvised."

"Besides him being a longtime friend, I only kept Vic around for entertainment."

"Nathan and I were also attacked the night we interrogated Vic."

"We'd had a fight; I sent a search party for him," Hades responded.

"I don't care about your relationship issues with a piece of shit like Vic. Tell me where the fuck Zeus is," I snapped.

Hades grit his teeth and swung, smashing his fist into the side of my face. My head snapped to the side and blood trickled down the corner of my mouth. I spit on the ground next to my feet and glared up at him.

"You had to tie me up to beat me. There's a word for people like you, Hades: loser," I snarled. I figured he hadn't gagged me because he liked to hear me scream.

Hades picked up the knife and jabbed it into my shoulder. The pain overtook me in a crashing wave. My vision blurred, and darkness settled in. When I came to, I was in a cell and freezing cold. The concrete dug into my knees and I huddled into a corner. I pressed hard against the brick wall, hoping I'd pass right through it. I was losing track of time. Hades would be back.

He'd beat me for killing Vic, and because he thought I would give him what he wanted in the end. The large cut on my thigh needed to heal faster. I was able to release one of my wrists from the tie handcuffs but the other wrist was broken and stained with blood. I had been badly beaten during the interrogation and I'd just pissed him off more when I wouldn't give him what he wanted.

I watched as spiders crawled into my cell through cracks in the walls. Big ones, small ones—all different colors. In they crawled, scavenging for food, then out they went. For a moment, I wished to be one of those spiders. My hope that I'd get out alive was beginning to disappear. I didn't know how Nathan and the others would find me, or if I'd ever escape on my own, and I wasn't sure which of Hades' multiple houses I was holed up in.

I was emotionally and physically drained. The temperature outside was dropping, which meant it was even colder in the cellar. I pushed myself to my feet, but when I took a step, my knees buckled, and I fell to the ground, letting out a yelp. The gash in my leg was deep and there were bruises all over my body. Footsteps came from the staircase and I looked up and saw Hades. I tried to move, but it hurt too much. Hades stopped in front of the cell door and stood there staring at me. Totally creepy. After a few endless minutes he unlocked the door and stepped inside.

I tried to get up, but my legs were too badly beaten. I saw Hades smile as he walked over. When he bent to pick me up, I backed up to the wall and he paused.

"You want to stay down here?" he asked.

"No, but if you try anything, I'll rip your fucking head off," I hissed.

Hades laughed wholeheartedly, doubling over. He carried me up the stairs and down a hall to the master bedroom; the room was dimly lit by candles. A fireplace on the far wall warmed the room and black couches sat in front of it. There was a dark, cherry four-poster bed on the other side of the room. It almost looked like an exact replica of Nathan's bedroom.

"Put me down," I growled.

Hades set me on the bed and backed away, leaning up against one of the pillars. "There's no use going anywhere. You can't walk," he chuckled.

The amusement in his voice put me on edge. He reveled in his power over me...well, he did for a moment. I mentally scanned the room, looking for a way out that would not ultimately get me killed.

"You'll never break me," I said.

He smiled and walked toward me, patting my cheek.

"Probably not, but I'll have fun trying."

I spit in his face and he grabbed my hair and yanked my head back hard. I yelped loudly. Hades flashed his fangs and brought his mouth to my ear. His breath on my skin was cold and wet, the smell of rosemary radiated off him like cologne. He was magnificently exotic; sexual urgency overwhelmed me, and he smiled horribly. This needed to stop. I wanted Nathan, not Hades.

"You're making it too easy for me to kill you, *ma chère*," he whispered.

He traced his tongue down my neck and reached his free hand up to caress my left breast. I grabbed his wrist and twisted hard. He yelped, and my nails dug in and pierced his flesh.

"Don't touch me!" I snapped.

I watched as blood fell from his wrist and soaked into the white carpet. What game was Hades playing? Something I'd learned about him: he always had ulterior motives.

"What's with the sudden hospitality? Are you going to sweet-talk me into your bed, get what you need, then kill me?"

Hades laughed. "You have it all figured out, don't you?" He walked over to the balcony doors and pushed them open. With his back to me, he kept talking.

"I have a proposition for you."

I got the impression that whatever this proposition was, it would cost me more than I would ever bargain for.

"And what is this enticing proposition?" I said mockingly.

He turned and faced me. "You stay with me; I'll tell you Zeus's location."

That perked me up. "And if I refuse?"

"If you refuse, your death will be slow, and I'll give Nathan the pleasure of watching. I'll give you twenty-four hours to decide. If you don't, I'll make the decision for you."

He walked over and bent down to kiss me, stopping just before our lips touched.

"Remember our bargain."

His lips touched mine and his energy seared through me. He turned and walked out of the room, quietly shutting the large wooden doors behind him.

Hades was not to be trusted, no matter how charismatic he was—I had to find a way out of here. Hades might tell me what I wanted to know if I agreed to the terms, but I wasn't willing to compromise myself to get the information. I'd just have to find another way.

Hades was playing games; he wanted to push me till I broke and agreed to what he wanted. Why did he want me with him so badly anyway? I stood and stumbled to the door, pressing my ear to it and listening to make sure Hades had left. When I figured it was clear, I returned to the bed.

I sat in the middle of the bed and drew in a breath, focusing all my energy, concentrating. I imagined the bedroom walls slowly disappearing, the cherry-wood bed evaporating. I envisioned myself outside in a garden, sitting on a brick bench surrounded by exotic flowers. I opened my eyes and the vision materialized before me. As my eyes adjusted to the bright sun I realized I was outside the castle walls. I had done it! I had transported myself.

My celebration was cut short by a blistering pain ripping through my head. Everything around me started to shift and disappear, like an apparition. My hands flew to my head—maybe if I squeezed hard enough the pain attacking my brain would subside. Frustrated and exhausted, I fell back onto the pillows on Hades' bed and let out a long breath.

"I need to get out of here."

I looked over at the grandfather clock, which stared down at me mockingly. My twenty-four hours were fast approaching. If I didn't find a way out soon, I may as well start writing what to put on my gravestone. My entire body ached—I was healing, but it was taking longer than usual. I sat up and examined myself. My hands weren't black and blue anymore, just a flushed red. The nasty gash that ran from the top of my inner thigh to my knee had begun to scar and dried blood dripped lines down to my ankle. My arms still showed signs of abuse; my wrist was destroyed, and large purple welts zigzagged up my arms toward the gash in my shoulder. I stumbled when I walked; my toes had been broken to keep me from running and I had to admit, that was pretty smart. I laughed—I looked like one big bruise—and I was stuck, Hades had made sure of that. He'd tortured me so I'd have to rely on him to nurse me back to health.

Even if Hades knew where Zeus was and I agreed to stay, he'd probably still kill me. He'd offered me a truce once before. Night came too soon; I had only a few more hours before Hades would expect an answer. Alone, my mind wandered toward my impending doom. I hated sitting here, waiting for Hades to kill me; I wasn't going out like this. I decided I should try to flash one more time. It would take most or all of my strength, but it was all I had left.

I figured with a lot of effort; I *might* be able to flash to the castle grounds. I tried, and when I opened my eyes, I smiled: it had worked. My body began to heal the moment I touched the earth, but even so, I was losing energy. I needed to sleep. Before the darkness took over, a vision of Nathan running toward me gave me a curious sense of peace. The last thing I saw was him leaning down to pick me up. He tried talking to me, but I could barely hear him. I think I smiled.

I OPENED my eyes languidly as the sun warmed my face. The softness of the cotton sheets cradled me lovingly and I snuggled in deeply...until the memories came back at full force. I jolted up, causing a mass of pain to shoot through my body. I looked around and instantly recognized the room: I had made it to the castle.

"You're awake." Nathan's voice was raspy and tired. He was standing in the balcony doorway. I cringed when I tried to move again.

"How long have I been out?"

"About a week," he answered.

He walked over and reached down to smooth my hair back

from my face. It was an odd sensation. Every time he touched me, a current ran through my body like a supercharged cable—it was addictive. His touch was gentle and welcome, and I leaned into it. He sat down on the bed.

"Can you tell me what happened?" he asked gently.

"To put it lightly, he beat the shit out of me," I laughed, then instantly regretted it.

"Lex, you don't have to be strong for me," he said.

I rose gingerly from the bed and braced myself on one of the bedposts. I was wearing one of his T-shirts. When my feet touched the ground, I stumbled forward, and Nathan caught me before my face hit the floor.

"You need to take it easy," he said.

I sat back down. That little bit of movement had exhausted me.

Nathan looked at me, surprised. "You're not going to protest?"

"I find that usually gets me into trouble. I do need to clean up, though," I said.

Nathan smiled. He placed his arms underneath my legs and behind my back.

"What are you doing?" I asked.

"You said you needed to clean up," he answered.

I tensed at first and Nathan noticed and instantly stopped. He stared at me, waiting for protest. Nathan had never done anything to me that I didn't want him to, so I just nodded.

He carried me to the bathroom, gently setting me down beside the tub. I grabbed the side for balance while Nathan turned on the water. As the tub filled, I tried to take my shirt off, grunting in pain. I was healing, but I still hurt. Nathan gently removed my shirt and tossed it to the side. I felt exposed in so many ways standing there in my bra and panties in front of him. The look on his face was pure predator. It excited me. His hands glided down my sides.

Nathan looked at me, his eyes asking me if I wanted him to

stop. I didn't. He traced his fingers over my stomach and a hitch caught in my breath. I bit my lip and quietly moaned. Nathan traced the lace top of my panties with his thumb, then crouched down to his knees and glided his tongue above the same stretch of skin. Another moan: maybe he was feeling the same intense heat when he touched me. I wanted him to take me right there, but I was fragile.

Nathan slid his hands between my thigh and touched the fabric of my panties. He pulled them down gently, careful not to bump against the open gash in my thigh, then reached around me and unhooked my bra. His eyes inked up—full black—and I couldn't understand the intense hold he had on himself. I thumbed my panties off, gently, and Nathan stood up. I held onto his shoulders and stepped into the tub with care. I sat down, the warm water on my bruised body felt like a relaxing hot spring.

I laid my head back and closed my eyes, savoring the moment. Nathan smoothed a washcloth over my skin, grabbed the soap and lathered, starting with my neck and finishing with my toes. His touch was like fire searing through my blood; it was something I had never experienced with another man. Dem had told me Nathan had feelings for me, but I'd been too scared to process it.

Nathan stood, and I did too, gripping the side of the tub. Nathan wrapped a towel around me, helped me out of the tub, and let me lean against him.

"Thank you," I said.

Nathan brushed my hair out of my face and smiled. "It was my pleasure."

Nathan helped me walk out of the bathroom and to the bed, then he backed away, leaving me feeling rejected. I paused for a second before wrapping my fingers around his wrist. He looked into my eyes and saw the same need inside me that was inside him. He began to kiss me but stopped. I waited for him to leave, to change his mind—and maybe I should let him to avoid passing the point of no return for the both of us.

His lips touched mine softly. I parted my lips and slipped my tongue between his teeth. The kiss was pure passion and a fire ignited inside me, my blood turning to liquid fire. Nathan stared down at me.

"I don't want to hurt you," he whispered.

"Then you'll just have to be gentle," I smiled.

Nathan hooked the bottom of his shirt, lifting it over his head and tossing it on the floor. The moonlight highlighted his every muscle, rope after rope of it, chiseled to perfection under his beautiful, lightly golden skin. Nathan unzipped his jeans and pushed them away. He was huge, just like I'd expected—long and hard as a rock. He grabbed my towel and removed it, tossing it to the floor. Then, he eased on top of me, caressing my cheek with his thumb. He bent his head down and kissed my bottom lip. I closed my eyes, luxuriating, breathing him in deep. He brought his lips and teeth to my neck and I leaned my head back and moaned.

Nathan traced his tongue down my neck to my chest and sucked my right nipple into his mouth. Pure ecstasy radiated off my body and I parted my legs. His body reacted, his erection gliding along my inner thigh. He lifted his head to look at me. It was my last chance to stop him, to tell Nathan I didn't want this. But there wasn't any reason not to keep going.

I raked my fingers through his hair as he guided himself to my center and slipped inside. I gasped sharply as he pulled out almost all the way and slid back in. A moan of deep pleasure escaped me. Nathan gained a little more speed each time he rocked inside me and the gates of Mount Olympus appeared before my eyes.

"I've wanted you since the moment I saw you," Nathan breathed heavily.

I touched my hand to his cheek and smiled. I brought his lips down to mine and kissed him deeply. Guess there was no going back.

I lay in bed, exhausted. Two times with Nathan had been so physically exhausting I wanted to stay in bed for a month. Reality hit me in that moment—the others would be curious. I sat up next to Nathan holding the sheet over my chest and smiled down at him. His eyes were closed.

"I know you're not asleep," I said.

Nathan smiled and opened his eyes. He reached his hand up and touched my face. I leaned into his touch and kissed his palm before gently putting my feet on the ground to stand. The pain in my body was gone. Maybe it was because of my ability to heal or maybe I was walking on air and endorphins. When I pulled the balcony doors open, a soft breeze floated into the room, lifting the sheet I had wrapped around my body. Nathan growled, which made me smile.

It was still night, but dawn was fast approaching. In the distance, between the mountains, the sun was peeking over the horizon. I sensed Nathan behind me. Setting foot in Greece had turned my life upside down. I'd kept Nathan at a distance, too afraid of my emotions and I wasn't sure what last night meant for us…or if there even was an *us*. The sun was beginning to rise. If I listened hard enough, maybe I'd hear the rays of the sun stretch out over the mountaintops. A moment later, it had engulfed the mountains in light.

"Lex," Nathan said, tearing me from my thoughts.

I looked up at him. He was incredibly beautiful. His blond hair fell around his shoulders, his strong jaw showed signs of day-old stubble, and his eyes had changed from their usual crimson to amber.

"Mmm?" My voice was almost a whisper.

He just stared down at me.

We both wanted to get back in bed, but we'd have to face the music sooner or later.

"I need to get cleaned up," I said.

Nathan grinned widely. "I can certainly help you with that."

I turned to leave, but Nathan caught my arm and turned me to face him. He kissed me deeply, grasping the small of my back and pulling me into him. The other hand tangled in my hair and he tilted my head to the side to kiss me deeper.

Knock, knock.

"Nathan?"

Nathan growled and pulled away from me in protest. I retreated to the bathroom and shut the door. I took a quick shower, wrapped a towel around myself, and walked out into the bedroom. It was my room and my things. I had attachments to everything. My favorite pair of jeans, the leather jacket that I felt naked without, and my boots. It's bizarre how sometimes you can be most at home when you are in a completely different place.

Nathan was gone, so I grabbed those jeans from the dresser and put on a royal blue off-the-shoulder top and my black boots. I put my hair up in a messy bun as Nathan walked in from the attached sitting room.

"Who was at the door?" I asked.

"Raider."

I was about to get bombarded with a million questions and part of me just wanted to crawl back in bed with Nathan and stay there while everything sorted itself out. I headed for the door, but Nathan stopped me. I looked up at him and he looked worried.

"You're still not fully healed. I don't want you to stress yourself out."

I touched his cheek and smiled. "I've spent a week asleep reliving every moment in that room."

I saw the internal struggle in Nathan's eyes but I didn't understand what it meant. He brushed the hair off my face and caressed my cheek. His caring touch warmed every part of me, but my insecurity reared its ugly head, leaving me exposed. Was he just being tender because we'd just slept together, and he didn't want to hurt me? I had never been in a situation that caused me so much fear. If he wounded me, would I ever recover?

"Lex, that's not true," he said.

"What are you talking about?"

Nathan laughed. "Your thoughts are written all over your face." He kissed me, and I was sure: this wasn't mere pity.

We headed downstairs and made our way to the entertainment room where everyone was waiting. Raider was leaning against the wall, pool stick in hand, waiting for Dem to shoot. Everything stopped when Nathan and I walked in.

Well, this is awkward. I didn't want to sit down—I'd been off my feet for days and I was afraid that if I sat, I wouldn't get up. I took a seat on the arm of the couch and waited for the questions to fly. I was healing, but my body still showed small signs of abuse—there was evidence on the side of my face where Hades had coldcocked me.

"Who's first?" I said with a laugh.

Everybody looked at me, surprised that I was making a joke at my expense. The silence was making me anxious and I was happy when Raider chimed in.

"What happened?"

"As you can see, I got the shit beat out of me," I answered sarcastically.

"Lex…" Nathan started.

I looked over at him and took a deep breath to calm myself.

"This is payback for what I did to Vic…and for spitting in Hades' face when he made a pretty vile proposition."

"What proposition?" Nathan asked.

"Hades offered up information on Zeus's whereabouts, in exchange for my soul."

It was accurate in a way, agreeing to stay with Hades would

mean I'd be forced to give up my freedom, something I was never willing to do. Even Nathan didn't have that type of pull.

"What did you tell him?" Raider asked.

I looked at him with surprise. Was he kidding? "Obviously I told him to shove it."

"Do you think that was a smart choice?" Raider asked.

"Excuse me?" I said incredulously.

"That's not what I meant."

I waited for Raider to clarify. *This should be good.* He was quiet.

"What did you expect me to do? If you haven't noticed, I'm one big fucking bruise. Excuse me for not thinking about *your* needs when I was getting the shit beat out of me," I said angrily.

Raider could be a real dick sometimes. Was it just me he had an attitude with? I was ready to spit fire. We were all under a lot of stress and we were certainly tired of playing games with Hades. Besides, even if I had taken Hades up on his offer, who's to say he would have given me the information I wanted? Oh, he would...on his own time. I shuddered at what it would take, though. Nathan noticed.

"You all right?" he asked, concerned.

"I think somebody just walked over my grave," I said.

I looked over at Raider. "Even if I had taken him up on his offer, there is no way Hades would have given up any information right away. We'd be stuck in the same situation we are in now. You might not think that's a proactive approach, but I'd still like to have my dignity and my life after this is over."

Raider was silent. Either he was letting what I'd said sink in, or he just didn't care. He had his reservations about me, but after a few months he should trust me at least a little. Raider and I were a lot alike; we trusted only those we were close with, those we would risk everything to protect. It reminded me of Marius. No matter what stupid shit we would get into—jumping off the cliffs in Avalon or getting into fights with those who thought I was favored over everyone else—he would always have my back.

Even if it cost him other friendships, we always had each other. I missed him so much.

Raider just nodded in response. That gesture was all I'd get from him, but I guess it was better than some snide remark.

"Hades said he wasn't behind the attack on the hill," I said to no one in particular.

"You believe him?" Dem asked.

"I don't know. There isn't anyone else who has the kind of power needed to bring those creatures through a portal. However, what would he gain from lying? What is it about me that he wants so bad? I feel like we're missing something. He was willing to give up Zeus but changed his mind when I came into the picture. Why? What am I missing?"

Everyone glanced at each other uncomfortably. Were they hiding something? Why?

"Hades will find out Lex has disappeared, if he hasn't already. I think it's time to update our security system," Nathan said.

I was beginning to get a headache. I wanted to sleep for days and forget about everything going on around me. Nathan must have noticed my internal turmoil.

"You good?"

"I just need to lie down," I said quietly.

Nathan herded me toward the stairs, but I stopped.

"Nathan, I'm okay. You don't need to come with me."

I wanted him to, but I was worried about the vulnerable state it would put me in. He nodded and reached up to touch my cheek. I saw we were alone and we kissed, pulling each other closer...ending upstairs in bed.

I loved watching Nathan sleep. He was beautiful. His strong arm was draped over my back and my head was resting on his chest. I listened to his heart beating, his breath steady. My whole body warmed. I felt safe and content.

I got up languidly. Nathan must have noticed the bed shift because he opened his eyes, looked up at me, and smiled. The looks of uncertainty on my face must've worried him. He reached up and touched my cheek.

"I know what you're thinking," he said quietly.

"Yeah?" I smiled back.

"You're thinking that this thing between us is just convenience."

Maybe, I said to myself. *That'd be easier.* I looked at him, frozen in fear. What if he agreed? In the time I'd been here, I'd started to fall for him. We fought incessantly and we hated each other in the beginning, but...my thoughts trailed off.

"Lex, whatever you're thinking, whatever you're afraid of, you don't need to be," Nathan said. "I know we haven't been each other's biggest fans but, along the way things changed."

"What changed?" I asked.

"The thought that I'd lose you..."

"When I was stuck in that portal, I was gone for a month," I said.

"I know you can face anything that's thrown at you, but Hades is different. He's manipulative and charismatic. He would torture you to death and you'd swear he was bringing you closer to heaven."

He looked away.

"I should know," he said.

What did that mean? Nathan wasn't much of a "let's talk about our deepest, darkest secrets" type.

He brought me down to him and kissed me. Our moment was interrupted by a knock at the door. I internally growled, but Nathan got up and answered it. Muffled voices conspired as I snuck into the bathroom for a shower. When I emerged, Nathan was sitting on the edge of the bed; he looked up at me when I stepped into the room. Whatever had transpired while I was in the shower wasn't good. Nathan filled me in.

"That was Dem. Apparently, Raider took off."

"So, why is that a problem?" I asked.

"He's sort of not in the right frame of mind to be taking off."

I was confused. Raider was a grown man, why was it such a big deal if he left the castle? Did he turn into a homicidal maniac after midnight? I said as much to Nathan and he chuckled.

"Something like that."

I just stared at him. Something was up and clearly I was out of the loop. Nathan had mentioned at Ares' place that Raider was different, but he didn't elaborate.

"If he's in trouble, shouldn't we go look for him?" I said.

"What do you mean *we*? You're not in any shape to be going anywhere," Nathan said.

"I beg your pardon?"

Nathan stared at me. "I'm not going to win at this am I?" He sounded defeated.

He needed to trust me; this would never work otherwise. I threw on clothes and walked out the door without waiting for him.

I met Dem in the foyer—he was strapped and ready to go. I looked behind me but didn't see Nathan. Not to sound selfish, but what did this have to do with finding Zeus? A few moments later he came downstairs wearing what looked like military gear.

"Are we going to war or something?" I said.

They looked at each other. Something was off.

"Someone going to tell me what's going on?" I asked, irritated.

"Raider's, uh, different..." Dem said.

"Apparently. He can't even go out at night by himself," I said.

They looked at each other. This was getting ridiculous.

"I thought we were supposed to work together?"

"He's a shape-shifter," Nathan said nonchalantly.

I paused for a second and remembered learning about them from Marius. Raider was a shape-shifter? I'd assumed he was a demon, like Nathan.

We piled into the SUV and headed into Plaka. I was starting to learn a lot more about this world and the "things" in it. It occurred to me that the only way to experience life was to be in it. Avalon was a place to find peace and protection, but the world was much bigger than I'd ever imagined—what else would I come across?

I was knocked out of my headspace when something hit the side of the SUV. The impact was so intense it made the car spin, then something hit the car from the other side, causing it to upend and flip. As we rolled, my head smashed into the passenger window a few times, the window shattering. Finally, I was thrown a few feet from where the SUV stopped. I tried to get up but was disoriented; I hadn't fully healed and my bones had shattered. Something grabbed me from behind; I tried to struggle from its grasp but failed. Then something hard hit me in the back of the head. Darkness.

———

I WOKE UP COLD. I felt like I'd been hit by a freight train and run over twice. I opened my eyes and looked up at a stone ceiling. I turned over to get a better look at my surroundings; I was in some underground room equipped with a cell door. Wonderful. My mind leapt to Nathan and Dem. Where were they? Were they okay? What the fuck happened? Someone moaned. Raider was on the ground just two feet from me. I sat up slowly and clutched my head.

"Raider?" He didn't answer.

I crawled over to him and turned him over. His eyes were closed, and he looked like he was in a lot of pain. I put his head in my lap and touched his face.

"Raider?" He opened his eyes and looked up at me. "Hey," I said.

He stirred, groaning. "What are you doing here?" he asked.

"We went looking for you."

"Well, you found me," he said sarcastically. "Where are Nathan and Dem?"

"I'm not sure. Something hit the SUV and we crashed. Next thing I knew, I woke up here."

"You're my rescuer?" he laughed.

"Yeah, so be grateful," I said.

"Whatever," he answered.

"Do you know what happened?" I asked.

He stood and walked over to the cell door, clutching the bars. "I was headed to Jen's bar when I was sideswiped by something. The car smashed into a tree and I was dragged out."

"What was it?"

"All I know is it smelled like rotting flesh," he shivered.

137

"You didn't see what it was?"

"I was too busy figuring out what the fuck was going on," he growled.

"Raider, calm down, it was just a question."

"Why don't you do something to get us out of this mess?"

"Like what?"

"Can't you flash?" he asked.

I looked around and touched the wall behind me.

"Not out of here."

"Figures," he mumbled.

"What is your issue with me?" I asked.

"You've done nothing but fuck everything up. Our best leads on Zeus are either in pieces or burned like a fucking crispy critter!" he snapped.

"Hey! You guys would be in the same place without me," I retorted.

"We're in the exact same place with you. Must be some sweet pussy for Nathan to keep you around."

Now I was pissed. An orange ball of fire formed in my hand and hit Raider squarely in the chest. It took me less than a minute to realize I'd made a big mistake. Raider dropped to his knees clutching his head. I watched as three-inch canines sliced through his bottom lip, heard flesh tearing and bones breaking. I walked deliberately to him and planted a hand on his shoulder. Raider jumped back and planted himself against the wall, his eyes turned completely black.

My eyes widened as I watched Raider change. His flesh tore over expanding muscles, his golden skin turned black, and his spine stuck out of his back. He fell to the ground on all fours, fingers turned into claws and a dragon-like tail whipped around the small room. He grew to the size of a horse and horns pushed out from the sides of his head.

Chairs scattered upstairs—no doubt whoever was up there heard Raider's transformation and the hell-demons that had attacked us at the castle came running downstairs, followed by, holy shit: Ares, who walked casually behind them. One of the demons unlocked the cell door and stepped inside. Raider was so fast—a blur. He slammed into it, ripping it in two. Ares threw Raider against the wall and stopped by my side.

"You were behind the attack at the castle!" I snapped.

Ares smiled. "You're getting too close, Lex. You don't even know what you're capable of." Then he disappeared.

Dammit! Raider regained consciousness and turned to face me.

"Oh...shit," I whispered.

I was looking at the creature I'd fought in the club the first night I was in Greece. Raider stalked toward me like the man he used to be. I froze. In a flash, he was right in front of my face. He wrapped his hand around my throat and lifted me off the ground, then he slammed me against the wall and bounced my head off the rock. Ouch.

"Raider..." I wheezed.

It didn't penetrate. He just licked his lips.

"Raider, it's me."

His eyes narrowed, and he cocked his head to the side. Caressing my cheek with his thumb, he turned my head to the left, exposing my neck. His tongue traced my vein; I felt sick. This wasn't the Raider I knew, and there was no way he was into me. It brought back memories from the night at the club. His hot breath filled my nostrils and he curled down to rip out my throat...

A second before he bit down, a roar echoed off the walls. Raider let go and I hit the ground hard. I looked up and saw Raider recoiling in a corner. Nathan loomed over me. I looked up at him and a scream yanked me back to reality. Raider rolled into a ball, naked; Nathan shrugged off his coat, wrapped it around him, and threw Raider over his shoulder. Loud grunting and footsteps sounded from the stairs—more demons were coming.

A lightning orb formed in my hands and I threw it at the fucking things. The force was powerful enough that they exploded when it hit them.

Nathan busted open the doors, which let out to an open field. A black truck was parked on a hill a few feet in front of us. Dem opened the back door of the double cab.

"What took you so long?" I asked Nathan.

Nathan's eyes flashed crimson. "Don't start with me, Lex."

"Ares was behind the attack at the castle," I said.

Nathan shot me a look of surprise. "Are you sure?"

"He came in right before you did."

"Did he say anything?" Dem asked.

"That I was getting too close," I answered.

"Too close to what?" Nathan asked.

"I have no idea."

Dem helped Nathan hoist Raider into the back and Nathan hopped behind the wheel to start the engine. As I climbed into the back seat on the opposite side of Raider, a horde of demons started running up the hill toward us.

"Are you in?" Nathan called, but the words didn't register. "Lex!" Nathan shouted.

I snapped back into focus. "Punch it!"

The engine roared to life and the car jerked forward. I watched the horde behind us disappear into the dead of night. I leaned back against the seat and took a deep breath. I was struggling with the fact that Raider was the creature I had run into—literally—that first night. And that Ares was behind the attack on the castle. What was his cryptic message? I knew less about this world than I thought. And how did Raider get like that? What causes him to change? Is it anger? Did he change because I hit him? How did he change back so quickly?

"You good?" Dem asked me.

I pushed the hair out of my eyes. I was tired of people asking me that.

"Just trying to sort things out in my head," I answered.

"Welcome to the freak show," Dem chuckled.

I was exhausted, and I leaned my head against the window. The memory of Raider's hot breath and his tongue on my neck startled me awake, we had just arrived at the castle. Nathan threw Raider over his shoulder as I opened the front door and followed them up the stairs.

Raider's room was different than Nathan's. It was masculine, but on every wall hung a weapon, things I'd never seen. A white leather couch and loveseat sat in front of a large marble fireplace and a black four-poster bed occupied the back wall. Nathan and Dem laid Raider on top of the bed, and Dem scrutinized me.

"Is there anything you can do?" he asked.

"Like what?"

"I don't know, enchant him with a spell or something?"

I raised an eyebrow. "Enchant him with a spell?"

Dem didn't say anything. He stared at me for a few minutes, then stormed out. I looked over at Nathan. He came up to me and touched my cheek and I leaned into his palm and kissed it.

"That was Raider, wasn't it? At the club?"

I walked over to the bed and looked down at Raider. He looked so peaceful, so quiet.

"I don't know what to do to help him."

Nathan was at a loss. I told him I wanted to stay with Raider until he woke up. There was much for us to discuss and I wanted at him first. Nathan nodded, and gave me a perfunctory kiss. He shut the door and was gone, leaving me to sort out my own issues.

I turned back to Raider, trying to untangle my tenderness for Nathan. I was falling in love with this man, a man who made me feel safe. He knew what I was, knew what I was capable of, and never used it against me. But how deep was his interest in me? I didn't know much about him—a frightening thought. He could be keeping things from me.

I had to push those worries aside and focus. I looked at the clock above the mantel; it was three in the morning. Raider's breathing was steady, his heartbeat normal. His facial construction was perfect: smooth golden skin, strong jawline, and shoulder-length black hair. I saw then why Jen was so attracted to him.

*E*xhaustion took over. I laid my head on the side of the bed, still holding Raider's hand. I woke up in a dark room, a small light pulsed to my left. I saw a massive beast cowering in a corner and a shirtless man standing over him with a whip in his hand. The man was yelling at the animal and the beast was whimpering and pushing itself deeper against the wall. It gazed at me with sad eyes. The man turned to face me: it was Raider. The look on his face was pure evil, his wicked smile making me cringe.

I was pulled out of the image and suddenly, I was lying on the floor, Raider on top of me, pinning me down. His eyes were black; he was trying not to change.

"What the fuck are you doing?" he growled.

I tried not to notice that he was completely naked. His hand grabbed my arms and pinned them above my head.

The bedroom door flew open.

"Hey!"

Nathan pulled Raider off me, throwing him against the wall behind us, then hurling his pants at him.

"What the fuck is wrong with you?" Nathan growled at Raider.

"She was in my fucking head!" Raider bellowed.

I stood up, rubbing my arms. "I'm sorry. I was trying to help," I said.

"Violating my mind is what you call helping?" Raider snapped.

"I said I was sorry."

"Wait, why were you in his head? What were you doing?" Nathan asked.

"I thought if I could separate Raider from the beast, he might be able to have better control."

"Have you ever done something like that before?" Nathan asked.

"Once," I admitted.

"And?" Raider and Nathan asked in unison.

"She lost control of both," I answered honestly.

Sealey. She and I had grown up together, with Marius. She was part elf, part banshee and very powerful. She taught me a lot about myself and my gifts, and she asked me to try to separate her two sides, so she could finally find peace. She kept begging me. No one else was able to help her so I gave it a try, against my better judgment.

When I touched her, I meant to give her some of my power so she would be strong enough to separate her two sides herself. Well, to make a long story short—it backfired. Now, she spends her time locked in a cell beating her head against the wall. I swore I would never do that to anyone again.

I said this to them, and both were quiet. I'd wanted to help Raider. I saw how he suffered and an indescribable need to help him overwhelmed me. Was I losing my mind? Nathan looked over at Raider, my guess was for permission, and Raider shook his head.

"I promise I won't do anything to hurt you," I reassured him.

Other than having another Sealey situation, the only thing

that worried me was the possibility of transfer. When I had touched Vic, he'd tried to use my power against me, and he ended up a crispy critter. Raider would never make that mistake, but I was worried that when I touched him something *else* would try to latch onto me.

"Raider, I won't force you to do anything you don't want to. I don't even know if it will work," I said again.

"What if it doesn't? What will happen to me?" he asked.

I looked over at Nathan, then back at Raider.

"I'm not sure," I said honestly.

"Worst-case scenario?" Nathan asked.

"The beast takes over completely, or you lose control of both parts of yourself," I said solemnly.

"It sounds crazy, but if there's no other choice, you can do whatever you have to do when the time comes," said Raider solemnly.

He said it with such conviction; he wanted to be able to control the beast, but he was afraid it would cost him more than he was willing to sacrifice. In that moment, Raider began to trust me.

"Deal," I responded honestly.

Raider smiled and headed toward the bathroom while I followed Nathan into the hall, stopping him once the door was closed.

"Do you feel okay about everything?" I asked. Even though I agreed to help Raider, I was still a little worried.

"I will always be there to bring him back," Nathan said firmly.

They were so protective of each other, what was their back-story? A few times I'd witnessed their animosity toward each other, but in moments like this, they were family. And what about Dem?

"One day you might not be able to."

He looked at me nervously. "Are you saying the next time he changes it could be permanent?"

"Nathan, I can't say for certain. Raider has obviously been like this for a long time. Why are you interested in changing him now?"

"Raider's been looking for a way to control himself. I guess I thought you might be able to do something."

"I don't have all the answers, but if the time comes, I can try to help him. You should remember that there are some things that can't be undone."

He sighed. "What a fucking mess."

"Nathan, I'll do everything I can, but I need you to be prepared if it goes south."

He nodded, kissed me, and walked away. I leaned back against the wall. What a fucking shit show. So much was going on that we were starting to get off track. Locating Zeus was hard! With the knowledge that Zeus was not my parents' killer, what was I going to do? Apollo had said Zeus wasn't the one starting this war, so what did that mean for my mission? If Zeus was innocent, why was he hiding?

My mind wandered to nothingness until it was interrupted by a commotion downstairs. It sounded like an army was invading the castle. I ran toward the sound and opened the door to the weight room, I wasn't prepared for what I saw. The whole room was in a whirlwind. A fucking portal had opened right in the boxing ring. What. The. Fuck.

Everything happened so fast. The portal had opened right under Dem, who had been using the free weights, causing him to fall. Luckily, he was able to keep himself from going all the way through.

"Hold on," I yelled to Dem. I looked around, ripped apart one of the ring's ropes , and threw one end toward him.

"This better fucking work," he yelled back.

I was hoping the very same. With all the loud noise coming from the portal I was surprised I could hear him at all. Suddenly, something hit me from the side, knocking me to the far wall. I held onto the rope with all my might. Portals are nasty little shits and my grip was slipping. I frantically looked around to see what had hit me and saw Nathan. His eyes were cold, completely void of anything.

"Nathan, what's wrong with you?"

He threw his leg out, kicking me in the stomach. The rope slipped from my grip, causing Dem to fall farther through the portal. I let out a loud grunt. Nathan was being controlled by something. He kicked me again and my rib shattered. A loud giggle reverberated from the portal.

I stared, astonished. The powerfully familiar little girl who had haunted my dreams stared at me. Behind her stood Ares. What the hell was he doing here?

Raider had finally decided to join the party—I guess all the noise made him curious.

Nathan was staring at the girl in some sort of trance. She lifted her arms and Nathan stepped up to the portal. I tried to stop him, but struggled because I was still trying to keep Dem from being sucked in. Fortunately, Raider was there. He reached for Nathan, then saw Ares and fell to his knees. He grabbed his head and the most bloodcurdling scream came out of him.

I looked at the girl. Her eyes were dead, soulless; it was unnerving. Raider wouldn't stop screaming and started changing into the beast. Great, we were about to be fucked. I turned my focus back to Dem and Nathan. Nathan was getting closer to the portal, so I knocked him into the wall with a bolt. I began pulling Dem out, while keeping my eye on the girl. She opened her mouth to scream and thousands of insects came at me, trying to make me loosen my grip. I hated bugs, but there was no way I was letting go. Oh Gods, they were crawling all over me.

"Fuck! Dem, I could use a little help here!" I yelled.

He got the gist and began pulling himself up. Wind was battering me from the open portal and disgusting creepy crawlers were trying to set up shop in my hair. Nathan was still knocked out and Raider had fully changed. My grip was about to fail when I saw Raider saunter toward me. Dem climbed out.

"Bout fucking time!" I yelled above the noise of the wind.

Dem shot me a death glare. He squared off against Raider and I started trying to figure out how to close the portal. It turned out I didn't need to; it started to close on its own the minute Dem got free. I looked into the eyes of the dead girl as it slowly closed on her. Raider did too, and apparently saw something there that caused him to go into an incredible rage—he howled and jumped through the stained-glass window. Great.

After a moment, I stood up, breathing heavily. "You good?" I asked Dem.

He just nodded. I walked over to Nathan who was sitting up, rubbing his chest.

"You hit me," he said.

"You didn't give me much choice," I responded.

"Are you all right?" he said.

I nodded and he just sat there, quietly.

"What the hell was Ares doing in there?" I asked no one in particular.

"Ares was responsible for the attack behind the castle, the attack in the cell where Raider and I were, and now this. The way I see it, he's getting closer to the end game. If Zeus isn't in on all this, we may just need his help to stop it. He's the only one powerful enough," Dem said.

I looked over at Nathan. "What happened to you back there?"

"Forget about it."

He pushed himself off the floor.

"How was a portal able to open right there?" I asked.

"I'm not really sure. I was working out, then *bam*," Dem said.

"Why did Raider go all beast mode?"

"Ares is the reason Raider is that way."

"What do you mean?" I asked. I looked at Dem, confused.

"Ares created him."

"For what?"

"To be used as a weapon."

I wanted to know more, but Nathan stopped me. "We don't have time for this."

"I'm going after Raider." Dem said.

"We'll catch up," I responded.

Dem nodded and headed out. It was just Nathan and I.

"I'm sorry I hurt you," Nathan said.

"Please. You've beaten me harder than that."

He chuckled softly.

"Nathan, whoever that girl used to be, she's gone."

"You don't understand," he said.

I sighed. "Nathan, you're going to have to face your demons— for lack of a better word— sooner or later. If you don't, it could get everyone killed."

He was silent. Life has a funny way of throwing itself in your face. It takes the most vulnerable parts; the things you don't like about yourself, and dangles them right in front of you as a constant reminder of your insecurities. I didn't realize then that this conversation had the power to change the course of my life. I had no time to drill Nathan on his issues. Raider was in the wind. What would we be up against when we found him? He'd been pretty pissed when I pushed into his head and saw him for what he truly was, saw a side that Raider had tried hard to hide.

I headed toward the front door, but Nathan took my arm. I looked down at his hand, then up into his face. There was so much emotion behind those beautiful eyes; his menacing demeanor melted away in that moment. He wanted me to blindly trust him; to be by his side no matter what we faced, to understand that he had secrets, and to accept he wasn't ready to face them. I reached up and touched his face. He slowly smiled and I became that person I never wanted to be: someone vulnerable.

Plaka is absolutely beautiful at night. The old buildings glow, illuminated by light posts that stand tall on the cobblestone streets. The sky is midnight black, making the stars shine ever so brightly. People were out celebrating in the bars, smiling and laughing. It made me wish I were as naive as they are.

Nathan and I walked side by side and I remembered the first time I set foot in Athens. I was so hell-bent on taking charge and so solely focused on my mission that I didn't notice how my life could be turned upside down. I was thankful for these allies I hadn't expected to find.

As we walked, I kept my guard up, listening to everything around me and focusing on finding Raider. You'd think with every corner of this place lit up, it would be easy to spot a massive beast, but no—he came at us like a freight train, taking us both down. Raider's beast form threw Nathan into the Chic Boutique on the corner while I flew through the Starbucks on the opposite side. I crashed through glass, flying over booths, tables, the cash register, and the coffee grinders behind the counter.

"Fuck!"

I stood up, brushing broken glass off my clothes and out of my hair.

"You're gonna pay for that, buddy," I said out loud.

I looked up and saw customers cowering behind booths. Raider came smashing through the huge hole he'd put in the wall, then sniffed around looking for me. He threw his large arms around, smashing the walls and scaring the few customers dumb enough to stay behind. Then, he focused his attention on them. I had to act. Their eyes were pleading for me to help.

I did the only thing that came to mind: I picked up one of the grinders that had broken my fall and threw it at his head. To my surprise, it smashed into a thousand pieces. A low growl from deep inside his throat made me shudder. He looked over his shoulder at me and grinned. I looked at the customers, expecting them to hightail it out of there...but they just stayed where they were.

"What are you doing?" I shouted. "Get the fuck out of here!"

They scrambled like cockroaches out onto the street, screaming and running in different directions. I had to get Raider somewhere safe before he made more of a mess. I flashed to him, coldcocking him in the face when I appeared in front of him. He fell hard, howling the whole time. I needed to make my move, so I sprinted past him, but wasn't fast enough. He grabbed me by my arm, and I screamed as it broke. Then, he threw me straight through the hole in the wall and into a light post, bending it at an awkward angle. I hit the ground, almost dizzy, then looked up to see Raider stomping toward me.

I got up, flashed, and clocked him again; blood spurted out of his mouth. He backhanded me, but before I ricocheted into another pole, I flashed and ended up behind him. When he tried to hit me again, I ducked out of his reach, jumped up, and kicked him in the stomach, flipping over and landing on my feet. *I think I just pissed him off,* I thought, as he bellowed.

Locals huddled by the windows and the doors of the shops watched the fight. Some, who were unlucky enough to be in the street, were running every which way, screaming. Nathan came out of nowhere, jumping on Raider's back and driving him into the ground. I watched as Nathan started to pummel him in the face. Raider just kept howling. At this rate we would tire out before we accomplished anything.

There was only one thing left to try. Raider had told me to do it if I didn't have any other choice.

"I have an idea," I yelled at Nathan. "Hold him still!"

"Are you kidding me?" Nathan yelled back. Raider was howling so loud I was surprised I could hear anything.

"Just do it!"

Nathan put Raider in a chokehold. I flashed to Raider's side and touched his temple gently. In a matter of seconds everything in Raider's mind raced through mine, his hopes, his fears. I grabbed onto anything that was man and ripped it from the beast. He fought me tooth and nail as Nathan struggled to keep his body still.

Suddenly, Raider was thrown from Nathan's grip and into the same light post I'd hit earlier. I didn't fare much better. My back hurt and my neck hurt—like every bone in my body had gone through a blender. When my head stopped spinning, I looked around and noticed I wasn't in the street anymore. I was on the ground in front of the post office down the street; one of the copy machines had broken my fall. I tried to move, but it just made me hurt more. I lay there, pathetic and outdone.

Nathan approached, talking on his cell phone, which he put in his pocket when he reached me. He was talking to me, but the pain made the words come through jumbled. I stood up slowly, bones cracking, and Nathan's words resolved. Raider had been knocked out, but at least he was himself; Dem was taking him back to the castle.

J opened my eyes and a bright light shined in my face, turning everything into oil. I closed my eyes and opened them again, trying to clear my vision. I was in Nathan's room. I tried to sit up but a sharp pain ran through me, making me gasp.

"You're awake." Nathan popped his head in the bathroom. "Don't move."

He didn't have to tell me twice. I was happy to be in Nathan's bed even though my arm felt like it was stuck in a vise grip. That's when I remembered what had happened: Raider had grabbed me by the arm, bending it in the opposite direction, causing it to break. I tried to assess the damage, but every move I made caused a ligament to tear.

Nathan came out of the bathroom holding a bowl of water and wearing nothing but dark jeans. Damn, he was gorgeous. Rope after rope of muscle enclosed in beautiful, flawless skin. His blond hair was pulled back in a bun. He walked over and pulled a chair to the side of the bed, taking my hand to wash the dried blood from my knuckles. It stung, and I pulled my hand back. He looked up at me.

"Sorry," I said.

"It's okay."

He smiled in a crooked way that gave me goosebumps.

I looked down at my attire—it wasn't my own. I was wearing yoga pants and a baggy white tank top with a sports bra. Had he undressed me? Had he noticed my blood-red bra and matching boy shorts? He read my mind.

"I asked Jen to pick some stuff up for you. She dressed you when you were out, since your clothes were covered in blood. She wrapped your arm, too."

He said her name with endearment. Had they been more than just friends? I didn't broach the subject, it was not my place to ask such intimate questions. Jen was beautiful in that old Hollywood way—timeless, but still sexy. An annoying jealousy hit me.

He finished cleaning my hands, stood up, and looked down at me. He opened his mouth to say something but didn't. I watched as he walked back to the bathroom, then I rose and walked toward the balcony. I opened the door; the breeze was warm and inviting. The sky was a mixture of oranges and pinks that reflected off the clear blue water of the ocean. I watched as the sun dipped behind the tree line. It was one of the most beautiful things I had ever seen; second only to Avalon. Home.

It seemed so far away from here—a lifetime away. Nathan came up behind me and part of me wished he would wrap his arms around me and tell me that everything would be all right… but we were a long way away from "all right." We kept getting sidetracked from the mission, things just kept happening. Would we ever find Zeus?

"Sometimes I forget how far we are from the rest of the world. How far you are from yours," he said.

I didn't turn around; I held the railing and took a deep breath. "It crosses my mind every now and then," I replied, then changing the subject. "We keep getting sidetracked and seem to be moving farther away from our mission. If it's true what Apollo said, and

Ares isn't the only one involved, why hasn't his accomplice showed his face? Why can't we find him? I feel like someone is dicking us around."

I turned and looked at Nathan. "Also, why does it matter whether humans live or not? They're vicious, vile, jealous creatures."

Nathan sighed, "I've lived for many years and I've seen what humans are capable of. It's true that they act out of fear, jealousy, and hope, but in the end, it's the humans who bring more life into this world. It's the humans who, when faced with adversity, will band together to protect what is important to them. We're not so different from them."

"Is that why you believe they're worth saving?"

Nathan stepped closer. He brushed a strand of hair out of my face and hooked it behind my ear. His hand rested on my cheek as he looked into my eyes—his stare was intense, soulful. He leaned in closer and I closed my eyes. His lips were the softest of velvet as he brushed them against mine. He was waiting for my permission so I opened my mouth and accepted him.

He caressed his tongue against mine, taking my lips bit by bit. It was the most intense connection I'd experienced. That one kiss packed in a lot—his hopes, his fears, and who he was as a man. Nathan pushed me back into the bedroom and I gripped the bottom of my shirt and pulled it over my head. He grabbed my hair and kissed me deeper, then picked me up and laid me on the bed. He trailed his hands down my sides and over my stomach, then caressed my breasts. My fingers wandered down his chest, teasing every inch of his hard body; a body I desperately wanted on top of me. Nathan stood, unbuttoning his pants, and I noticed he was going commando. He climbed onto me, peeled my pants off, and threw them on the floor.

I pulled his head down and kissed him with more urgency. He kissed my neck and gently made his way to my breasts. He sucked in one nipple, making it hard, and turned to the other, lovingly teasing it. I gasped at the sensation running through my body: heat. He kissed his way down my stomach, placing butterfly kisses over my hips, as I raked my fingers through his hair, a few strands falling around his beautiful face. Then, he bent his head lower and my legs parted while I frustratingly waited for what I wanted. One flick of his tongue and my body arched; I gasped loudly as he explored my body, licking and sucking. My hands twisted the sheets, ready to tear them into pieces because he was taking his fucking time. He teased me, bringing me right to the point of release and pulling back.

He looked up at me and licked his lips—his eyes were solid black and I saw something behind them. His true self, maybe. His demon. He crawled up my body and hovered over me, and I arched closer to him, ready to take him. He slid into me gently.

Nathan was rocking back and forth, and I had an ineffable feeling of tenderness—as though everything was fitting into place at that moment. He looked into my eyes and I saw myself in his; my whole world looked back at me. It was as if I was watching my life play out through the eyes of someone else. It was something I had never experienced before. Nathan watched the same show, looking through me without being present. When it was over, he kissed me.

The bed shifted and I wrapped the sheet around me and got up. I found Nathan on the balcony, looking out into the ocean. Should I approach him or leave him alone? I have an inquiring mind, so I stood beside him and followed his line of sight. The ocean was quiet and calm.

"I watched your entire life play out right before my eyes. I'm trying to understand why," he explained.

"I wanted you to," I said. I had wanted him to see my life in Avalon; my friendships, my sadness, my moments of happiness. If we were going to be together, he needed to know everything. I showed him that cold place inside me, the place that sometimes made me feel invisible and powerful, like I risked completely losing myself. It used to scare me. Not anymore.

Nathan turned and faced me. I explained to him why this was so important to me: "If we can trust the information we've gotten so far our reasons for searching for Zeus have completely changed. I don't know what I'm supposed to do, and I'm worried you're keeping things from me. What are you afraid to tell me?"

He said nothing for so long. Then, to my surprise, he walked past me, put his shirt on, and walked out, slamming the door behind him. My bedroom was only a few feet from Nathan's, but I retreated and took a shower to clear my head and heal the small ache in my heart. I needed to leave. After I dried off and dressed, I tied my hair back in a high ponytail and visualized where I wanted to be. Raider came in at that moment and I saw his eyes bug out as he watched me materialize into nothing.

I found myself walking out of the alley behind the bar. The activity from last night hadn't left an imprint on the locals; scaffolding had been placed around Chic Boutique and Starbucks, and I barely saw anything as I walked down the street. People walked by in fast-forward while I remained in my head, trying to sort out my emotions.

I'd never expected to get close to anyone and it terrified me. I didn't have a destination; I just kept walking. Someone called my name, but I didn't care—I needed some space.

After what felt like hours, I looked around to see where I was: the hill of Zeus's temple. How fitting. I would walk in and face him the only way I knew how: I'd confront his statue.

His representation sat on a gold throne, radiating power. Statues of the kings of the animal world were carved out of the same precious stone. The Zeus statue wore a toga draped over one shoulder and around his lower half. He held his mighty spear and gazed over a reflecting pool at his feet. Giant columns lined the walls, with plush seating at their bases. It was beautiful. His stone stare went right through me, wondering what I was there for.

The place was empty, which was fine with me—I needed this time alone. I sat on one of the seats, facing him with my back against the column. This magnificent being would either be my victory or my demise. Oberon wanted me to kill him but with everything I'd learned—if it was even the truth—how could I? A small part of me felt a twinge of regret, in the event of victory, and I was not sure why. I leaned my head back against the column and closed my eyes.

My night with Nathan ran through my mind; I played a continuous loop of the moments before he stormed out. I wanted to be with him, but I worried about his secrecy, and for some reason, there was a part of me that wanted to stay away from him. In the end, I was only hurting myself. I didn't know how to go on; I had never been in this type of situation.

A noise from the entrance of the temple startled me. I looked around the column, trying not to draw attention to myself, and sighed with relief. Worshippers were coming to pledge everything they had, hoping for their prayers to be answered. I stepped down from the seat and headed for the door. People were kneeling before the mighty statue and as I passed, I just shook my head. Gods brought nothing but trouble. "Good luck," I mumbled.

"*Apistos*," an old man said.

I was jolted into the moment. "Excuse me?"

The elderly gentlemen looked up at me with determination. There was something unusual about him, like he was far more powerful than he let on.

"You should not be here if you are going to speak blasphemy," he said.

I stepped closer to the old man and he rose slowly. His beautiful crystal-blue eyes stared at me, and a sense of familiarity crept into my heart. It reminded me of the little girl from the portal. I shook internally.

"Do you really think he cares about you, old man? Do you think your hopes and your prayers will somehow magically solve your problems?"

I saw something change in his eyes and he stared at me with sadness. I cocked my head to the side, trying to read what he saw in me. He smiled. Were those tears in his eyes?

"My child, all any of us have left in this world is hope. If we lose that, then we may as well not exist."

"Hope is for the weak. You can lose yourself waiting for something that is just a means to an end." An end even I'm afraid to meet.

He reached his hand up, placed it on my cheek, and smiled.

"As can you," he said quietly.

He turned and knelt, continuing to pray. The old man seemed to know what was going on around him and for some reason I felt a kinship with him. *That's odd.* It had been a powerful, calming exchange and as I walked out of the temple, I considered what he had said.

My life had started to change the moment I came to Greece, whether I wanted it to or not. I closed my eyes and flashed back into my room. I walked into the hallway and descended the stairs… hearing the sound of yelling and things being thrown against the wall. I approached the weight room and opened the door to a hundred-pound weight hurtling my way. I was quick enough to duck before it smashed through my face. All three guys stared at me and Nathan stomped toward me. What was he going to do?

"Where the fuck have you been?"

"I needed a break," I said.

"You should've said something," Nathan snapped.

I got in his face; I was no one's property.

"You're not my keeper," I said.

"Where your head's been lately, you need me to be."

"I'm not a child Nathan, I don't need to tell you when I leave."

This thing between us was clearly not going to work. A couple nights of passion aren't going to change the fact that we are both stubborn and set in our own ways. We would fight to the death for those around us, but together, we still obviously had trust issues. It hurt more than I wanted to admit, but that's how it was.

We stared at each other until Raider cleared his throat. I looked over at him, thankful for the break from Nathan's disapproving stare. Raider walked toward me—even in a massive room he was intimidating. Well, the beast side of him was.

"I'm sorry. I heard I hit you pretty hard," he said.

I laughed. "I think the worst of it happened after I touched you."

He looked at me quizzically. "Yeah, I want to ask you about that. Can you explain what happened? I don't remember much."

"I was able to separate you from the beast, only for a moment, to get you under control."

"It was the weirdest thing. I think you did something to me," he said. "I don't know how to describe it. It was like I was in your head and I saw your parents' death. I felt everything you did."

I glanced over at Nathan. How was that possible? I hadn't injected myself into his subconscious like I'd done the first time I touched him.

"It happened to me too," Nathan said. "Last night."

Raider got the gist—we'd been together overnight. He smiled and winked at me and I rolled my eyes.

"What does it mean?" Raider asked.

Everyone looked at each other, not sure what the answer was.

"It's called transference...a reproduction of emotions relating to repressed experiences, especially of childhood and the substitution of another person," said Dem, who was on his computer looking up the definition.

"In layman's terms?" Raider asked.

"Your emotions are so close to the surface, Lex, that any kind of contact will cause the other person to see flashbacks. You've opened yourself up too much."

I started to pace the room. I needed to learn to control my emotions before they got me or someone else killed. They were traitors, waiting to be used against me. I stayed in my headspace for a few minutes, unaware of what was going on around me until a soft touch grazed my shoulder. I looked up into Nathan's eyes and what I saw surprised me: understanding and regret. What did he regret? I didn't have time to process it. I backed away from his embrace and saw hurt in his eyes.

I looked over at Dem. "What can I do?"

The look on Dem's face told me that whatever it was, I wasn't going to like it. He sighed.

"You need to forget."

"I have tried to forget the worst day of my life. It's not as easy as flipping a switch," I said.

My irritation was starting to show. They wanted me to forget everything that made me who I was. Raider had gotten a quick glimpse, but it wasn't as intense as what Nathan saw. The tension in the room was weighty and thick. I heard a noise behind me and turned to see Jen standing in the doorway.

"Why are you here?" I snapped, sounding sharper than I meant to.

Jen shifted her eyes to Nathan, then looked right back at me. She cleared her throat before she spoke.

"I got here this morning. Some of the girls haven't shown up for work the last few nights. After what happened to Serene and Jules, I started to get worried when I couldn't reach them on their cells," she explained.

What had Apollo said? The prostitutes were payment. If Zeus wasn't a client, maybe Hades was. I figured Jen kept her clients confidential, but Hades seemed to fit the profile. Maybe he'd be willing to talk. There was only one way to find out.

"Don't worry Jen, we'll figure out what happened," I said. She smiled and asked Dem to give her a ride back to the bar. Dem walked past me and gave my arm a squeeze. He followed her out of the house, and I watched as they got in the car and drove away. I started to walk toward the front door.

"Hey! Where are you going?" Nathan called after me.

"I'm going to talk to Hades."

Nathan walked toward me.

"Do you really think that is going to go well? He kidnapped you, tortured you, and now you're going back to him?"

Was Nathan jealous? "He hasn't come after me yet," I said.

Nathan looked back at Raider, who just shrugged.

"She has a point," Raider said.

Nathan turned back and I smiled triumphantly. He ran a hand down his face and looked up at the ceiling.

"Alright, but you're not going alone," he said. I wanted to respond, but Nathan continued. "Raider and I will go too. We'll stay far enough away that we won't be spotted, but close enough to help in case you get in trouble. If you refuse or take off on your own, I will throw you in the cells."

The tone of his voice made it clear he was serious. I was silent, and he took it as a small victory. *Well, well, Nathan—you won this one.*

"Fair enough," I said with a little uncertainty. I wasn't sure if I was ready to go face-to-face with Hades.

After I got ready, I found Nathan and Raider waiting for me by the door. Whatever happened tonight, something told me things were going to change and my stomach sank, like I was about to jump off a cliff. I used to love that sensation, but right now, not so much. I was on the verge of change, but would it be for the better or for the worse? It was time to take a leap of faith.

Nathan called Dem to fill him in and the look on Nathan's

face told me that Dem was not so sure it was a smart plan. I really didn't care. We piled into the SUV and for the first time I wondered, *Geez, how many cars do these guys have? Where does all their money come from?* We sat in silence the entire way, navigating to another one of Hades' properties that the guys had located while I'd been stuck in the portal.

I was alone in this, but maybe there was a way to compromise. Yeah, that would go over really well. If I proposed a compromise, Hades' response would be some sleazy remark about him giving me the answers if I got on my knees or on my back. I snorted. Nathan looked at me in the rear-view mirror; I guess I had been a little louder than I intended.

"Are you sure about this? He might not give you what you want," Raider said.

"Not for free, anyway," Nathan mumbled. I sensed jealousy in his tone.

The closer we got to Hades' home, the more nervous I grew. I was going into the lion's den with a fat slab of meat hanging around my neck and all I needed was a dinner bell. Nathan parked a block from the house and we filed out of the car like soldiers. Nathan turned, his mouth a flat line. No one else had come up with a plan—not a good one anyway. Raider made sure the coast was clear while Nathan stared at me for what seemed like forever, not saying a word. He was about to say something when Raider ran back to us.

"It's all clear. Doesn't look like you'll run into an ambush, but I can't be too sure."

I laughed without humor. "Thanks."

Nathan spun me toward him and went in for a kiss before stopping himself.

"Just…" he began.

"Don't do anything stupid?" I finished for him in a joking manner. Nathan wasn't amused. He looked worried, and honestly, it made me more nervous.

He sighed heavily. "Be careful."

I smiled. "Have you ever known me to...?"

"Don't finish that," he cut me off.

I headed off toward the house, aware that both sets of demon eyes were drilling holes into my back. If Zeus didn't want to start a war, his asshole brother Hades seemed like a prime suspect.

Hades' home was definitely not what I'd expected; it wasn't dark and freaky like something out of a cheesy horror movie, on the contrary, it was pristine and elegant. The beautiful two-story structure was white with two columns on each side of the door that held up the huge balcony on the second floor. Large windows adorned the front and the top story, looking out on a generous emerald-green lawn that looked as if it had been recently mowed. The brick walkway to the front door was dark-gray stone, the two steps to the porch were cherry wood, and the porch wrapped around the house. The door opened at my knock, and Hades stood before me, looking powerful and sexy as hell. Nathan's gorgeous, and Hades doesn't compare to him, but Hades is downright hot! His wicked smile touched me in places I longed to be touched.

"What a wonderful surprise—a beautiful woman knocking on my door. To what do I owe this pleasurable greeting?"

Ugh. He was sexy and charming, but he never knows when to quit.

"I'm here to talk, Hades, so you can get your mind out of my pants."

I tried to sound short and disinterested, which was difficult around him. His smile faded for just a moment, but it was back just as quickly. He opened the door wider and stepped back, inviting me in.

"Of course, my dear. Please come inside."

I stepped into the house and kept my guard up. The door shut with a soft click, but I didn't hear a bolt lock—he wasn't keeping me here. The foyer was white marble with flecks of black and red. Two staircases wrapped from the front entrance to the second floor where a balcony overlooked the entryway. The stairs were red velvet, the railing black. I looked up at the high ceiling where a gorgeous chandelier hung. One of Hades' hands palmed the small of my back as he held out the other to escort me to the library.

"Come, we can sit and enjoy a drink while you tell me why you have come to my home."

I followed him to the library, keeping my distance so he wouldn't accidentally—or not—bump into me. If he noticed, he didn't acknowledge it. To say that the library was beautiful, was an understatement. The entire room was filled top to bottom with books—rows and rows wrapped around the room. Ladders to the top catwalk rolled on perfectly polished wheels. I found myself agog. This room was unlike anything I had seen in my entire life. Hades laughed behind me, and I turned around, noticing the grin on his beautiful face.

He sat tall in a red-velvet wingback chair and I took a seat across from him. He stared at me with such intensity that it took all my willpower not to squirm. The smile never left his face, even when he called for his butler to bring him a glass of wine and raised his glass to me.

"Can I offer you a drink?"

I was getting impatient. "No, thank you."

Hades nodded to the butler, who left through the side door and I dove right in.

"You seem awfully calm about me being here," I said.

"Why wouldn't I?" he asked.

"Oh, I don't know? Maybe because the last time I was at one of your shithole homes, I was trying to escape."

"I would appreciate it if you would refrain from insulting my belongings. Besides, I no longer required your presence."

He was so nonchalant about the whole thing that it made me

worried. Something was going on that I was missing. How the fuck was he so calm?

"You tortured me because I killed Vic. Or did that slip your mind?" I snapped.

"True, but I'm over it now. Tell me why you're here. If it's because a few useless prostitutes went missing, you're looking in the wrong place."

How the hell did he know about that?

"I have spies everywhere, Lex." He sipped his wine, tracking every breath I took. "Who is spreading these terrible and false rumors? Oh wait...must be your lover."

"This isn't about what Nathan believes or doesn't believe, it's about what I want to know."

He set his glass down and sighed. "What makes you think I know anything? Do you think I have them locked in my cellar?" he chuckled.

"As a matter of fact, yes I do."

He finished his drink and set the glass down. His face turned serious. "Lex, I have never kept anyone against their will. Except you, maybe."

He smiled. Anger boiled inside me.

"I'm a manipulative bastard, but I don't need to resort to kidnapping to get my jollies off."

I raised an eyebrow, but he waved me off.

"However, I might have some information that you'd like."

I waited impatiently while he stewed on my anxiousness. I was starting to fidget; my foot was jiggling on the carpet, my hands were playing in my lap. I wanted to throttle the bastard.

"I don't have all day to sit here and play games with you," I snapped.

"To be honest, I don't know where Zeus is. I faked that knowledge as a ploy to get to you. Rumor has it he's building an army to bring war and destroy mankind."

"I've heard all this. However, I've also heard the rumors are just that: rumors. That someone else is trying to bring about war. And you know what? I think it's you."

Hades laughed. "That's a good one. Alas, you'd be wrong. I happen to adore humans. It's no secret I hate Zeus and given the chance I'd do anything in my power to see his head on a spike, but I have no need or want to destroy humans. Besides, it's not Zeus I'd be worried about."

"Why not?" I asked.

"Because 'Zeus's daughter will bring eternal darkness,' so says the prophecy, in so many words."

"Zeus's daughter is dead," I responded. Hades fell silent and stared at me for what felt like several minutes.

"Not true," he said.

"How do you know?"

"I'm staring right at her."

14

Now it was my turn to be silent. I was so stunned by Hades' words that my mind fumbled around, trying to comprehend everything he'd just said.

"What the fuck are you talking about?" I was trying to stay cool but failing miserably. Was this another game?

He convulsed with laughter, "This keeps getting better."

I flashed, straddling him and holding a knife to his throat. He was so shocked, he knocked his glass on the floor and it shattered.

"What the fuck are you talking about?" I growled. What the hell was going on? Was any of it true? Was my whole life a lie? Why didn't I remember any of this? How is this possible? Why didn't Oberon tell me? Did Marius know? There were so many questions running through my mind.

He tried to swallow, but I dug the knife in a little deeper and silver blood dripped down the side of his neck.

"Do you mind?" he growled.

His eyes turned black and he glared at me. I eased up on the knife but took my time crawling off him.

"I will not be threatened in my home. Thanks to your lack of manners, this meeting is over. When you learn more respect, I will tell you what you want to know."

He stood and proceeded to walk toward the staircase.

"Lawrence can show you out."

But I am the most stubborn being I know, besides Nathan. I planted my feet; I was not moving without answers. Big mistake. Hades materialized before me in a flash of gray smoke. His left hand was around my throat; he squeezed so tight my hands scratched at his wrists trying to get him to let me go. My feet dangled at least two feet off the ground.

"Do not mistake my hospitality for weakness," he growled.

The tone of his voice made me want to shrink into myself, but I didn't show it. He loosened his grip and set me down. The rage was still in his eyes, and though it was dissolving slowly, he still seemed keen on ripping my head off. As he let me go and stepped back, I saw his restraint was beginning to wane.

"Get out of my house. Come back when you have better manners. And if I were you, I would do a little more research on who I was spending my time with."

With that, he was gone and Lawrence came and showed me to the door. I walked back to the car, navigating a thousand questions. If I was truly Zeus's daughter, why hadn't Nathan told me? Why hadn't any of them? How was I going to approach this?

I had gone to Hades with a plan, but now my world was beginning to crumble. I tried to come up with a reason why Hades would lie—he hasn't been the most trustworthy character so far, so…the truth could be almost anything.

I reached the car much too fast and Nathan and Raider were waiting, worried looks on their faces.

"How'd it go?" Nathan asked.

"Fine."

It wasn't a very satisfying response, but what else could I say? Did I trust Hades? I certainly felt different in Greece, but is a vague sense of familiarity evidence of a whole other life I don't remember? I climbed in the car, numb to everything around me, trying to even start to understand. How could I go on, knowing that everything from this moment on would change? I was angry, hurt, and scared. My heart beat faster and my skin grew tight and sticky like it wasn't its own. I searched my cold place to find the truth. Was it hidden somewhere, too deep for me to grasp?

Nathan kept trying to talk to me, but I ignored him. Everyone had kept things from me; hatred and betrayal pumped through my veins. I wanted to grab his head and squeeze it till it popped like a grape. That image made me smile. I must have looked crazy to Nathan because when I noticed him looking at me, his eyebrow was raised. I turned and looked out the window, watching the world go by in apparent slow motion. I was exhausted and had every intention of getting back to the castle and crashing.

We drove in silence; every now and then I would catch Nathan looking at me. He was wondering what had happened, but he could sit and stew a little bit longer. We made it back to the castle around two in the morning. When the car was parked, I jumped out and hurried to the front door but Nathan caught hold of my hand, a look of concern in his eyes. We both waited for the other to say something and when he didn't speak, I started for the door.

I stormed up to my room; Nathan didn't follow. It was better that way. There was already too much swirling in my head and just the thought of his touch made me sick to my stomach. It's weird—when you open your mind, it can change everything. Something deep inside told me Hades was being honest. That cold place took me back to the image of a young woman standing with Oberon and Zeus. Her face was obscured the first time I had seen the vision, but now I saw her as clear as day: she was me.

I walked over to the balcony doors and threw them open. There was a slight breeze in the air—not too chilly, but just cool enough to chase away the anxiety running through my body. The sky was magnificently dark, with stars shining so bright that I felt like I was stuck in another universe. The ocean below was calm, so flat that the moon and stars mirrored back on the surface.

My head was still spinning, still trying to find the ground. Was Hades telling the truth? I wanted to confront Nathan about the secrets Hades had hinted at.

The thing was, did I want to know? My interest was definitely piqued, so I took a deep breath and decided to seek Nathan out. I couldn't hide up here forever, even though I wanted to. Before I reached for the door, a knock sounded on the other side —Nathan.

Nathan will always be gorgeous and intimidating. He took up the entire doorframe; there was no way of avoiding him now and honestly, I was tired of trying. I needed to make my peace and move on.

"We need to talk," Nathan began.

Straight to the point. This should be fun. I stepped aside and let him in. Thank the Gods the balcony door was open. Just having him in my room sucked the air out of my lungs and made the space seem extremely small. He was absolute power. He turned and faced me, looking as though he was holding back his emotions.

"Did Hades give you what you wanted?"

"Um, not really. He doesn't know where Zeus is."

Nathan raised an eyebrow. "You believed him?"

"What does he gain by lying to me?" I asked.

Nathan laughed with abandon. "Are you that fucking stupid?"

This time I was ready to *actually* pop his head off his shoulders. "I beg your pardon?" I said, aghast.

He stopped laughing. "I'm being serious, are you really that stupid? What does he get from lying to you? He gets you."

I was too pissed to sit down, so I paced the room. "What are you talking about?"

Nathan sighed heavily. "He gets you where he wants you. You trust him, and he'll use you for his own purposes."

I looked him straight in the eye. "Isn't that what you're doing?"

Nathan paused, confusion radiating off his face. "What?"

"You were looking for Zeus because of what the prophecy said. Now we know it might not even be true but that clearly doesn't matter to you. Why?"

He was quiet for so long I wasn't even sure if he would answer me. He raked his hands down his face.

"It's personal."

"That's not good enough," I said.

He looked at me with suspicion. "What does it matter to you?"

It was time for a different tactic. "Hades mentioned the prophecy involved Zeus's daughter."

Nathan was motionless. "What else did he tell you?" he asked.

"That I'm that daughter."

He sighed and I followed him out to the balcony. After a few moments he validated my fear: I was indeed Zeus's daughter.

"I don't understand. How is that possible? How are you involved?" I asked, confused.

"That is something you need to ask Zeus," Nathan answered.

"Well, we can't find him at the moment, so you answer me. What do you want with him?"

"He took my life." Nathan's voice was quiet, sad in a way.

"What do you mean?" I asked.

Nathan placed his arms on the railing while I stood beside him, waiting.

"He took everything away from me because I couldn't protect his most prized possession: his daughter," he said.

15

*N*athan kept his gaze on the water in front of us. The sun was rising over the horizon. So many questions swirled in my head.

"Why don't I remember any of this?" I asked.

"Lex, there are things I can't answer for you, only Zeus can," he said.

Even while I understood Nathan didn't have all the answers, I felt betrayed.

"Why didn't you tell me?" I asked

"Raider, Dem, and I weren't really sure it was you at first."

"I don't understand," I said.

"You weren't around Olympus all that much. You were probably younger than you are now, but it's hard to gauge how old immortals are. Zeus didn't want his affair to be public knowledge…although, it had never really stopped him before."

He uttered the last statement with sadness, reminding me of the girl I'd seen in the portal. Nathan was unwilling to tell me who she was.

"Go on," I said.

"Oberon was Zeus's most trusted advisor. However, he

wanted the throne for himself. He convinced some of the Gods to rise against Zeus. Oberon had plans to kidnap Zeus's daughter and take her to Avalon if Zeus didn't concede."

"Where do you fit into all this? And why would Oberon kidnap Zeus's daughter?"

I couldn't think of myself as her; it was too fantastical. It would mean my entire life was a lie and my parents weren't my parents…at least, my father wasn't.

"When Zeus found out about Oberon's plan to overthrow him, he tasked me with protecting his daughter."

Nathan paused.

"What happened, Nathan?" I asked.

"When I found her, there was nothing left of her. I'm not sure what happened. Best guess? One of Zeus's enemies found her."

This was a lot to process and I was still on the fence about whether I believed it all. Who could?

"As soon as we realized who you were, we tried to figure out how Oberon managed to bring you back and erase your memory," he said.

The night breeze started to pick up and the air turned chilly. Was Zeus listening in on the conversation, wherever he was? Lightning blazed in the distance, the stark-white tentacles reaching out to grab hold of anything in their way. A loud snap crackled throughout the still night and Nathan and I looked at each other.

The night sky turned bright white; it was like something had burst from thin air, blinding me. I held my hand up and covered my eyes. I was thrown inside the bedroom, hitting the back wall. Everything moved in slow motion. Nathan picked himself up off the floor and had started to help me up when both Raider and Dem broke down the bedroom door.

I lay immobile on the floor. The sight was too startling: Zeus, in all his glory. I must have hit the wall pretty hard because it was difficult for me to grasp what was happening. Was I awake or dreaming? The next few moments blurred in front of my eyes. Nathan punched Zeus square in the jaw—pent-up aggression, I figured. The punch didn't move Zeus an inch, and he struck Nathan back just as hard. Nathan ended up back on the floor.

Before I knew what was happening, Zeus had his hand around my wrist and I saw Nathan try to grab me. In a flash of white, I was pulled from the room. The look on Nathan's eyes worried me: fear. I saw fear in his eyes, and to be honest, I was a little freaked out myself. We were rushing through a tunnel, a black void with no air and no light.

I landed on my feet on solid ground, looked around, and noticed we were at Zeus's temple. Zeus had let go of my arm and stood before me in the flesh. I had no idea what to think, feel, or do. My first instinct was to get the fuck out of there, but my stubbornness got the best of me. We stared at each other, each waiting for the other to say or do something.

"Guess we can call off the search party," I said, sarcasm dripping off my tongue. What a great way to start the conversation. He just stood there and stared at me. "There must be a point to all this," I sneered.

He just stared.

"Seriously, you're starting to creep me out," I said.

I had to admit that, when he broke into a smile, it was very easy and charming.

"I apologize. I'm trying to grasp the concept that you're standing here." His voice was soft, but commanding. "You're different than I remember," he finished.

I was quiet. He stepped closer and reached out his hand to touch my face. I took a small step back and he nodded, smiling again. I saw inside myself the person I thought I wanted to be but never would; a soft-spoken woman who had never seen death or evil in her life and who was constantly happy. I had long ago given up trying to find a resemblance to that person.

"Why did you bring me here?" I asked.

"To tell you the truth," he responded.

I laughed. "You had to kidnap me to do that?"

He cleared his throat. "Nathan and I have had our differences in the past."

"Differences? That's not how he described it. He said you ruined his life."

"He lost my child!" he yelled, so loudly that the sky shook, and lightning crackled in the background.

"That was a long time ago, and obviously I don't remember any of it," I responded

"You might not remember, but I do. You never forget the loss of a child. It is a void you can never fill."

"You've got, like, a million kids. Why am I so important?"

"I don't have a million kids," Zeus responded.

"That's not the point," I said.

"You're powerful, Lex."

"All Gods are powerful." Acknowledging I was a God...weird. Did I really say that? Did I believe it?

Zeus sighed. "With me and your mother's blood running through your veins, you're an unstoppable force."

"What are you talking about? My mother was human."

"No, Lex. Your mother was a titan."

I was shocked. What was I hearing? I was so confused about who I was that my head spun. It was trying to figure out if this was all real. "Why didn't I know this?"

"Your mother wanted to keep the affair from her lover, Cronos. If he knew, he would have killed you, so Selene—your mother—went into hiding in Avalon."

"What about the man she was married to? My father?" I asked.

"He was a council member in Oberon's court. There was a secret wedding to hide who Selene really was, and to justify her pregnancy."

"Hades said Oberon killed my parents. Is this true?"

Zeus nodded.

"Why?"

"Cronos found out about the affair between your mother and I and learned where she was hiding. He ordered Oberon to kill your mother—and you—as punishment. But Oberon couldn't kill you because he wanted to use you to get to me."

"Why would he want you?"

"Oberon was my trusted advisor. We'd been through hell and back, and never turned our back on one another. If I was no longer able to fulfill my duties as king, I would hand the throne to him. But he became greedy. He began spreading lies that I wanted to eradicate the human race, and when one of my imperial guards warned me that his provocations were turning into an uprising, I fought. The war cost the lives of many, and unfortunately, my enemies were greater than my allies, so I fled. When the Gods still loyal to me found out the truth of Oberon's betrayal, they banished him to Avalon forever."

"Tell me what happened after your daughter disappeared."

"When *you* disappeared. *You* are my daughter."

I didn't argue with him.

"What happened?" I asked again.

Zeus walked over to the pool in front of his statue and looked into the water. He turned around and was quiet.

"I sent you to Tartarus to hide until I could send someone to find you. Nathan, Dem, and Raider were my imperial guards. They returned with news that you had been kidnapped, or worse," he explained. "My hatred and rage consumed me—I thought that I had lost you. I couldn't see straight. Oberon, my most trusted advisor, had betrayed me. My daughter had been taken from me. When I knew it was over and I'd lost everything, I traveled to Tartarus and hid there for years, keeping out of sight. Hades was the only one who knew my true location."

"Oberon sent me here to stop you from starting a war. It was only *after* I decided to take the assignment that he told me you were responsible for my parents' murder."

Zeus looked at me and laughed without humor. "Figures. He took almost everything from me. All that's left for him to take is my life."

"Why should I buy all this?" I asked.

"Look inside yourself for the truth, Lex. You have been lied to your whole life. You only have yourself to trust. Everyone else can come later."

I looked out to the water, engrossed. Was I this different person? Had I lived this different life I have no memory of? What was I like? Did I have a lot of friends, or was I a loner except for Marius? Marius. I wonder if he could tell me.

"I've felt different here. Like a part of me has been asleep for a long time, and it's just now waking up," I said. "And what about Marius?"

"I sent Marius to Avalon to watch out for you in case Oberon got too close."

"Who is he?"

"He was one of my imperial guards."

For some reason I wasn't shocked. So much information was being thrown at me, I could only listen. I searched inside myself for that dark place, but it was quiet, like it was absorbing it all too.

"Marius and I grew up together—explain our history."

"The young Marius you grew up with was an illusion. You needed someone to trust, to be close to, who would guide you through your life in Avalon."

"Does Oberon know about Marius?" I asked. I was afraid if Oberon found out that one of his enemy's former guards was living in secret in Avalon, Marius and his family would be in danger.

"No. Oberon does not know."

"I can't believe Marius kept this from me." Anger boiled inside me and that dark place wanted me to return to Avalon and punish him for what he'd done.

"Marius did it to protect you. If you need to hate someone, hate me. You needed to find out the truth on your own and make the decisions you needed to."

"Why did you come back? You've been missing for a millennium."

"I found out you were alive." It was a simple answer.

"Why did Oberon lie to me? Why did he send me to hunt you down and kill you?"

"If you killed me, you'd never have learned the truth."

"He must have known that in sending me to Greece, in sending me after you, there was a risk I'd learn everything."

"He made you think I killed your parents and wanted to start a war to bring about an end to mankind, but he underestimated you."

I brushed the hair out of my face. "I underestimated him too," I said with a sigh.

I stared up at the moon. The air around me felt cleaner, lighter; my whole life had changed in a matter of seconds. What do I do now? Do I return to Avalon and hunt Oberon down? Or wait till he comes to me?

"There is one other thing you need to know, Lex."

I looked up at Zeus. His crystal-blue eyes stared at me with sorrow.

"There is a prophecy of a second war."

"I know, I've heard: 'When the kingdom of light lies with divine power, it will be the end of mankind,' or something like that. Just not sure what it means."

"The prophecy is about you."

"What are you talking about? Are you saying I'm going to destroy mankind?"

Zeus was silent.

"That's ridiculous. How am I going to do that?"

"Oberon sent you to kill me. If you had been successful, your powers would be limitless—giving Oberon the perfect opportunity to use you."

"Use me for what?"

"To rule over the Gods and eradicate mankind. As we speak, Oberon is building an army with Ares at his back. He's rallying allies who are still loyal to him. That girl killed at the temple was to throw you off."

The cool breeze touched my skin lightly. This whole mission was a cover-up; a way to use me against Zeus and start a war just because Oberon feels entitled. I wanted his head.

"We need your help to stop Oberon and Ares," I said.

"I'm not sure the others will be willing to involve me."

"Let me take care of them," I said.

16

One minute we were in the temple and the next we were back in my room in the castle. Nathan was pacing while Dem and Raider tried to calm him down from their perch on the couch. When Nathan saw us, he attacked, hitting Zeus square in the jaw before the God had a chance to block him. Zeus was thrown against the wall and plaster crumbled around him. Nathan walked over.

"You all right?" he breathed loudly.

"Yeah."

Raider and Dem were on their feet, ready to move if needed. Zeus got up and I turned around.

"You deserved that," I said.

Nathan lunged toward Zeus, but I grabbed his arm.

"Don't," I said.

He looked down at my hand, then back up at me.

"Let go." His tone was threatening.

"Nathan, you're not going to touch him—and neither are you two," I looked over at Dem and Raider, who were about to take their own shots at Zeus.

Nathan looked stern. "Give me a good reason."

He was being an ass. I understood his reasoning, but the attitude wasn't helping.

"We need his help."

He looked at me, annoyed. "What for?"

"Oberon is building an army. The prophecy says the daughter of Zeus will bring about the end of mankind and Oberon wants to use me as a weapon."

"How do you know the prophecy is about you?" Dem asked.

"Because of who my mother was."

They knew who I was talking about; they had been Zeus's imperial guards after all.

"How is Oberon going to use you as a weapon?" Nathan asked.

"If I kill Zeus, his powers transfer to me. My mother was a titan and Zeus is my father—that's a lot of power Oberon is willing to do anything to get his hands on."

"He'll be after the throne next," Raider said.

Even with the guys on board, we needed more help. With Ares backing Oberon, we needed someone just as powerful as Zeus—I was willing to make a deal with the devil.

Of course, when I told Nathan my idea, he just said good luck, which is how Zeus and I ended up standing in front of Hades' door without the others.

I looked over at Zeus beside me. Would I ever comprehend that he was my father?

"This isn't gonna go very well," I said.

"I expect not," he answered me.

I knocked on the door, unsure of what to expect. Hades cracked the door and smiled when he laid eyes on me, but when he saw Zeus, all hell broke loose. Anger radiated off him in waves.

"Fuck!" he bellowed.

Flames burst around him and the impact of it hit so hard, it threw us fifteen feet. The doorframe was scorched and the look in Hades' eyes told me I was on his shit list too. I watched as Zeus launched himself at Hades, but it took me a second to get up, smoke sizzling in my lungs. They burned when I coughed, like my insides were on fire. I felt weak. Most of my energy was spent trying not to hurt my lungs any more by keeping my breath quiet and shallow. Tears streamed down my face.

I was able to look up and see that Zeus and Hades weren't in front of me anymore. Good thing Hades lived hundreds of miles away from civilization—the house was nearly destroyed. Laying on the ground allowed me to gather the energy I needed to take off toward the house.

I listened to locate them, but the house was eerily quiet. I crept through each room, being careful not to turn a corner at the wrong time and get myself killed. Noises rose from the basement and I started walking downstairs, noticing it looked more like another house than a dank cellar. The basement was large, with brick walls and dark-wood floors. There were spacious rooms set off to the side, some with their doors shut. The rooms that were open, looked like adequate living quarters—with large beds, dressers, couches, and fireplaces.

A loud crack came from the back of the basement. I sprinted across the room and was nearly at the door when a bolt came flying toward me. Just then, something hit me from the side, almost knocking the wind out of me. The bolt shot past and blew a hole through the wall where I was standing. I looked up to see what hit me and saw Raider's dark eyes. He stood up and held his hand out.

"Now we're even," he smiled at me.

I looked around for Nathan.

"He's coming through the back. He told me to get you out."

I looked up at Raider and lifted an eyebrow. He just smiled down at me.

"That's what I told him."

I peeked around the corner. Zeus and Hades were still on

each other. I knew they hated each other, but shit, man—they both had numerous burn marks and Hades was missing his left eye. A bolt hit Hades square in the chest, making a gigantic hole near his heart. It was a little disturbing and also fascinating to watch as the muscle beat steadily. Zeus didn't look much better; his right arm was charred and hanging on by a thread and half his face was unrecognizable.

We had to find our opening. If they killed each other before Nathan got here, we were fucked; we probably couldn't stop Oberon with just one of them, much less neither of them. I had a plan. It wasn't smart, but I had nothing left.

I flashed beside Hades, then gripped his arm and held on, trying to drain his energy. His black eyes turned on me, pouring hate and disgust into my veins. He smiled and long fangs grew before my eyes. He threw Zeus against the wall—or should I say, through it—then slammed my back against another wall, his hand tightening around my throat. I stuck my finger into his missing eye socket and he screamed. He responded by grabbing my wrist and snapping it in half. Now, it was my turn to scream. It was the worst pain imaginable.

Nathan flashed in, pulled Hades off me, and got one good hit in before he too was thrown like a rag doll. Hades grabbed my other arm and wrenched it behind my back. He slammed my back against his chest and licked my ear. Nathan, Zeus, and Raider closed in as Hades wrapped his fingers tighter around my throat.

"Uh-uh, Nathan. I'll rip her pretty little head off," Hades snarled.

Hades' hand traveled down the side of my face to my chest and he dipped his hand down the front of my shirt and into my bra. He caressed my breast and sucked my earlobe into his mouth. I tried hard not to make a sound, but it was incredibly erotic. Hades chuckled.

"You almost had me, Lex, but now I have you all over me."

He made his way down my stomach to the top of my jeans. He was close to reaching inside my pants when I forced all my power, or what I had left, into him. I drained quickly, but Hades' grip was slipping; he screamed, dropping me on my broken wrist.

Nathan and Zeus ran over and pulled me up. We stared as Hades grabbed his head and fell to his knees, then watched as his body was engulfed in flames. They pulled me outside, but I broke free and started running toward the house; it exploded, and I skidded to a stop, turning to Zeus.

"Want to tell me what that was all about?" I asked him, almost out of breath.

"Hades has hated me for eons—sibling rivalry. He believes I stole the throne from him."

"Do you think he's aligned himself with Oberon?" I asked.

"Hades doesn't play well with others. If Oberon is after the throne, there is no way he would help him. Hades will show his face again soon enough."

"I'm surprised to see you," I said to Nathan as he walked up to us.

"I figured something would go wrong and I'd have to save your life," he said with a smile.

I pushed the hair out of my face. "You were right."

Raider walked up and looked at everyone. "Now what?"

Hades would have been a good asset, but we didn't have time to wait around for him to grace us with his presence. I was still hoping to get him on our side, I just wasn't sure how I'd go about doing it.

"We need to regroup," Raider said.

Nathan started for the car, but Zeus and I decided to flash back to the castle. I regretted the decision a little—it would have been entertaining to see an all-powerful God ride in a double-cab truck.

We were greeted at the castle by Dem, who'd stayed behind in case Jen called. We agreed—Nathan, rather reluctantly—that

Zeus would stay in one of the spare rooms. It just seemed easiest to have everyone in one place in case something happened—but testosterone and immaturity were running high and it was making me feel claustrophobic. I headed for the garage and jumped into Nathan's Mustang. He walked up and leaned into the window.

"Where're you going?"

"I'm going to see Jen and get some fresh air. Don't kill each other while I'm gone."

Nathan was silent.

"I mean it. If anything happens to him while I'm gone, I'll leave, Nathan," I said with honesty.

"All right," he sighed.

He leaned over and kissed me. It was unexpected and I was relieved we weren't on the outs anymore. He caught my mouth and kissed me deeper, his hand behind my neck. When he pulled away and stared at me, something in his eyes changed. Whatever he saw in mine, made him smile.

I pulled out of the driveway and headed for Plaka. Apparently, Nathan and I were back on, but the big question was Hades. He's a God and virtually can't die, but I was curious as to what had happened back at the house. The only thing I was sure of was that when Hades resurfaced, he wouldn't waste any time looking for me.

Plaka was alive with locals and tourists alike out enjoying the warm air. The amber glow of the gas lamps danced with the music coming from inside the restaurants and I parked the car in the alley and walked through the back door—it was busy tonight. A live rock band was playing for a standing-room only crowd. I walked up to the bar—Jen was talking up a customer on the other side, but another bartender came over and offered me a drink. While he was pouring my beer, I sensed eyes on me. I surveyed the space but didn't notice anything out of the ordinary.

At the last second my eyes landed on Hades. I'd expected him to show his face soon, but it hadn't even been a few hours. Jen made her way over and noticed the shocked look on my face. She touched my arm to get my attention, but I shook her off. I. Was. Fucked.

He stalked toward me and without looking away, I told Jen to call Nathan. I didn't know if she actually would, and to be honest I wasn't too worried about it. I just had to get Hades out of the bar before we ruined Jen's livelihood. When he reached me, everything else became white noise and all I focused on was him; some part of him scared me shitless.

"Should we take this outside?" he asked rather smoothly.

He took my hand and led me to the alley. The door closed behind us and I was knocked to the ground by a hard right hook I didn't even see coming. That cold place inside me wasn't even paying attention—obviously, I was having an off day.

My head hit the dumpster, cutting my eyebrow, and I landed on the asphalt. Blood flowed down my cheek and I watched as it pooled on the ground. I was knocked out of my stupor and stumbled to get up, using the dumpster as leverage. Hades grabbed the back of my head and lifted his knee into my face, then grabbed my hair and threw me to the ground. My collarbone broke with a sickening crunch.

"You fucking bitch!" he yelled, and kicked me in the stomach.

I groaned loudly. Man did that hurt!

"You show up on my doorstep with that fucking piece of shit!" he said, his voice growing louder.

"I thought we could..." I coughed "work together." I was trying to catch my breath and talk too—it wasn't working well.

He turned on me, furious. "You thought wrong."

I rolled out of the way of his incoming kick and started to crawl on the ground, wading through Gods know what. I was running out of strength. Hades crept up behind me and knelt on top of me, pulling my hair back and exposing my throat.

He got close to my ear and whispered, "I wish I could see the look on Nathan's face when he finds you."

Hades kissed me without passion as he slid the cold knife across my throat. My face dropped onto the dirty, smelly street.

I'm not sure how long I was lying there. Laughter rang out from the entrance of the alley; late-night partiers, enjoying life without a care in the world. I tried to look around, but everything was blurry and darkness was closing in.

That cold place inside was giving me enough strength to stay awake. This was not how I was going out—lying in nasty, foul-smelling water in an alley behind a bar. My mind was trying to wrap itself around something. I faintly remembered talking to Jen and telling her to call Nathan. Maybe he was on his way, or maybe I'd imagined the whole thing.

I slipped away a few times, but my body began the slow process of healing itself—a dubious prospect with so much blood loss. With enormous effort, I pushed myself onto my back, but it only caused more blood to rush out of my open throat. My shirt was warm and soaked all the way through; my own blood keeping the chill from my bones. Time slowed down and I looked up at the faintly shining stars. They were calling to me, asking me to come play with them and from my position laying there, that was all I wanted to do. Maybe the stars had the power to make the pain go away, make everything disappear.

Someone brushed the hair out of my face and I saw Nathan's worried eyes watching me, his lips moving soundlessly. He picked me up, being careful not to jostle me, while Jen placed her hand over my throat and rushed me to the car. Then darkness inevitably took over.

IT HAD BEEN three days since my run-in with Hades at the bar. On the way to the castle, my body healed itself—somewhat. The cut in my neck was so deep that I kept bleeding out before it had time to heal. Raider and Dem kept watch to make sure I didn't bite the big one, constantly changing my neck dressings. Nathan spent the entire time I was out of commission looking for Hades. Apparently, Nathan had run into him while he was looking for me and a huge fight ensued. The bar got the brunt of it, along with Hades' other eye, half his face, and an arm, I'm told. The bar was closed for repairs, which is where Raider and Dem were at the moment.

The first thing I did when I woke up was get into the ring. Now, I was in the gym sparring with Zeus—it seemed like he and Nathan had come to some sort of understanding while I was incapacitated but I wasn't sure what that understanding was because neither of them would talk about it.

My mind was racing. Will Oberon come after me? I'd pretty much gone AWOL, so it was only a matter of time. And Avalon, was it still my home? Was it ever in danger? I'd inadvertently thrown enough power into my punch to launch Zeus backward.

"Hey!" he yelled.

"Sorry."

I took the boxing gloves off and wiped the sweat off my brow. I sat down on a chair in the corner of the boxing ring and put my head in my hands.

"You need to let it go. If you let him inside your head, you'll lose everything," Zeus said.

I laid my head back against the ropes. He was right. I had to keep Hades out of my head; he was insidious enough to destroy me.

"Thanks," I said to Zeus. A slight bond was forming between us. It was mystifying, since I didn't remember anything from my past life—is that what you'd call it? Zeus smiled and nodded. I walked upstairs for a shower. I was starting to feel whole again. My body had taken a major blow; I'd put it through too much and I wasn't sure what my next move would be. I never imagined

Hades would resurface so quickly; I guess I'd underestimated him.

Tomorrow would be different. The best way to handle anything was to be direct, but I had to admit, Hades had gotten into my head. When I was recovering, he was always on my mind, and to my sheepish surprise, most of my thoughts were of his hands touching me. It was a little too erotic—visions of intense pleasure that changed to complete horror, some of which would last for days. The worried look on the guys' faces told me I might be going crazy.

I wiped the moisture from my shower off the mirror and stared at myself. I was a complete mess; pale, with bloodshot eyes surrounded by dark circles. I walked out of the bathroom and there was Nathan, waiting for me. He laid his hand on my cheek and slowly glided it down to my throat. He gently touched the scar that hadn't quite healed, then put his lips to it—a kiss to make it better.

Passion and love was behind the kiss and behind his touch as he guided me to the bed. He gently laid me down, but I took control this time. I straddled him, bowed down, and kissed him deeply. He grabbed my hips and I kissed down his chest, wrapping my hand around his shaft and caressing him.

Nathan moaned and shifted. I looked up into his eyes and saw that they were black. His demon was at the surface and he was doing everything in his power to keep it at bay. I took him into my mouth, twirling my tongue over the tip of his cock. My mouth glided up and down as my hand kept pumping. I was bringing him close to the edge, and I was enjoying it. Nathan reached down and gripped my hips hard, flipped me over onto my back, spread my legs, and pushed into me. I let out a gasp as he pounded into me. I clutched his back—he was moving inside me harder and faster. I took it all—no pain, only exhilaration. This time he brought me to the edge, and I screamed as I climaxed, followed by Nathan. He collapsed on top of me but rolled to my side so as to not crush me. He lay next to me with his arm wrapped around me.

I was too restless to sleep. All those images of Hades wreaked havoc on my brain when my eyes were closed. I slipped from Nathan's arms, quietly got dressed, and padded downstairs to the exercise room. The whole place was quiet. Jen had taken up residence in one of the empty rooms while the bar was being fixed, and I'd noticed Raider going out of his way to make sure she had everything she needed. His attentiveness was maybe a little too much, but she was a grown woman, she could do what she wanted.

When I walked in the gym, the clock read four in the morning. I grabbed the hand wraps on the table by the heavy bag and wrapped up. I desperately tried to keep my mind clear, but with my lack of sleep, it was out of control. I accelerated my speed as I punched and kicked the heavy bag. I kicked it so hard it broke off the chain and smashed into the wall.

"Better?"

I turned around and saw Nathan standing at the door with his arms folded across his chest. I watched him walk over, pick up the heavy bag, and throw it over his shoulder. He stepped inside the ring and rehung it.

"Come on, again," Nathan said as he held the bag still.

I started punching the bag, trying to stay focused. I'd started to drift when Nathan punched me on the shoulder. I looked up at him.

"Stay focused." He sounded a little impatient.

I started again, making sure my body was fluid and it struck me that even though I had been training for years and was awesome at what I did, there was always room for improvement. It only takes that one moment for someone to catch you off guard. A part of me felt like a failure. *How will I be of any use to anyone if I'm not even strong enough to take care of myself?* That thought spurred me on; I was determined to get my shit together.

Nathan and I spent hours training. Then, he handed me a pair of boxing gloves and put on his own.

"Alright, no more practicing. Show me what you've got."

I raised an eyebrow then hit my gloves together. He started out with a right hook, which I dodged smoothly. One, two, three punches to Nathan's face. He ducked, then gave me an uppercut to the jaw—I stumbled back but caught myself before I fell. Several hours must have passed because Raider and Dem had come downstairs to watch the show.

"Two hundred bucks she wipes the floor with him," Raider said.

"Make it two-fifty," Dem replied.

I looked over at Raider and Dem. I couldn't believe they were making bets about which one of us would eat it first. I was surprised that Raider was on my side.

I peeled off my tank top and stood in my sports bra and workout pants. I lunged at Nathan again, but he caught my wrist with one hand and punched me with the other. Blood spurted out of my nose and I picked up my discarded shirt and wiped it off. We circled each other around the ring. When he got close, I flashed behind him and threw a punch that caused him to fly across the ring.

"Ooohhh," Dem and Raider both cringed.

Nathan caught himself before he hit the wall, looked up, smiled, and was on me again before I'd caught my breath. He threw punch after punch, landing a few on my cheek and jaw. I didn't come up short though; he threw a punch and I ducked, then threw out my leg and tripped him. His back hit the floor hard, causing the ring to shake. I looked down at him and held out my hand to help him up. We were both breathing hard and sweat dripped down my back. I looked over and watched Dem hand two hundred and fifty dollars to Raider. At least they'd given me a chance. I looked back at Nathan.

"I need to take a shower."

I left the ring and headed toward the stairs. I expected he'd follow me—he'd been wondering what was keeping me up at night—but he didn't. Maybe he figured I needed some time. I finished up and found Nathan waiting for me in the bedroom.

"Do you wanna talk about this morning?"

I sighed. "Not really."

"Tell me anyway," he said patiently.

I turned to the closet to get dressed, dropped my robe, and chuckled at Nathan's appreciative growl. I slipped on my black-lace bra and panties, a pair of skinny jeans and a long black tank. I put my hair in a loose bun, allowing a few strands to fall around my face. Then, I turned back to Nathan, who was leaning back against the bedpost waiting.

"I haven't been able to sleep. Every time I close my eyes the only thing I see is Hades' face. I hear screams, I hear laughing, and all I see is blood. Blood everywhere." I started pacing. "It's like watching a bad rerun and I can't turn it off. I don't really remember what happened back in that alley but everything's different now."

I stopped and looked over at Nathan.

"Like what?" he asked.

Nathan shifted uneasily.

"All I can focus on is him. I fall asleep and he's there."

Nathan grunted.

"Do you think I like having him in my head?" I asked.

I wanted to end this conversation. Maybe it was a mistake, bringing Zeus to the house. I'd also made a mistake by not watching my own back.

"Look, Lex, if you don't get your head right, you'll find yourself in a situation you won't be able to get out of," Nathan said.

"You think I don't know that? You think I don't realize I fucked up?"

"I didn't say that, Christ!" he was starting to raise his voice.

We dropped the conversation about my nightmares. Nathan

was right, I needed to find a way to clear my head. We headed downstairs toward the unusually noisy kitchen. Raider, Dem, and Zeus were sitting at the island drinking coffee and talking about Gods know what, and Jen was taking pots and pans out of the cupboard to cook breakfast. I walked over and poured myself a cup of coffee. I loved coffee—it had a weird aftertaste, but gave me the satisfaction that I needed.

"Do you want any help?" I asked Jen.

She looked at me and smiled. "Thanks, love, I got this."

I grabbed my cup and joined the guys at the table.

"We're heading to the club tonight I take it?" Dem asked. He observed me, sadly for some reason, then averted his eyes.

Raider glowered, asking, "You sure you can do this?"

I understood their hesitation. They trusted me enough to let me make decisions about my life and even entrusted me with theirs, but they were just concerned. I didn't intend to be a liability.

"Don't worry about me."

Raider smiled and nodded his head. He stood up and poured more coffee in his mug. He pinched Jen's butt and she turned and lightly smacked his shoulder. Raider caught me looking and winked. The others were too involved in their conversation to notice the camaraderie between them. When I looked at Nathan, he was staring at me.

We planned to hit Club Olympus around eleven when it got busy. Nathan said we were going to meet someone who was willing to help us stop Ares and with much protest from Raider, Jen offered to help.

"I don't think so," Raider said, pushed his chair back, and stood.

It was Jen's turn to speak and she got right in Raider's face.

"This isn't up for discussion, and I dare you to get in my way."

Raider looked at the rest of us for backup but Nathan and

Dem just shrugged their shoulders and Zeus paid very little attention to what was going on in front of him.

"She has every right to get involved, and frankly I'd rather not get in her way," Dem said.

Raider looked to me, hoping I would be the voice of reason.

"I have to agree with Nathan and Dem on this one."

I looked over at Zeus. "You're awfully quiet."

He looked at me. "I don't have anything to say."

I raised an eyebrow. "Really?"

I noticed Nathan and Zeus exchanging looks, but when they caught me watching, they averted their gaze. I didn't say anything at the time, but soon, I'd find out this was the turning point for everything. I would come back to this moment and ask myself why I let it pass without question.

Jen finished cooking and placed a plate on the table for me. It looked delicious, though I didn't have much of an appetite.

"You need to eat," Jen said.

"Jen…" I began.

She met my eyes.

"I'm starting to think that what happened to Jules and Serene also happened to the others." She sighed, "Raider told me everything."

She continued down the table, placing a plate in front of everyone. No one looked hungry, but they indulged her just the same and we ate in silence. *The calm before the storm*, I thought.

"I should head out," Jen said.

Raider gave her a quick kiss on the cheek, and she was out the front door.

"Leave the dishes, I'll get them later," Jen called.

Seemed to me she'd turned into a permanent resident. The clock above the sink read two in the afternoon. My head was still racked with images of Hades and I rubbed my forehead. Everyone was on edge and I was getting a headache. I stood up from the table and walked out of the kitchen and up the stairs without a word. The end of the hallway wrapped around, opening to another. Windowless stone alcoves stretched from the floor to the ceiling, lining the right side of the wall. Each alcove had enough room for a cushioned seating area. I stepped up, taking a seat on the bench and looking out toward the sun. I touched my healing neck.

I felt Nathan before I saw him. He sat on the bench next to me looking out toward the ocean.

"Everything that's wrong with this world makes me wonder if we can ever get sanity back," he said.

"Is it hard to imagine?" I asked

"In a perfect world? No. However, this isn't a perfect world," Nathan said.

"What world is?" I responded.

In the everyday human world, there is only one race of beings. When you look past your self, you can see that there are far more beings in the universe than humankind could imagine. All you have to do is open your eyes; a difficult task for some.

"I guess I didn't realize how different this place is for you. It seems natural for you to be here," he said.

"Thank you?"

Time had flown by. Sure, life meandered at a different pace in Avalon, but looking back, I remember bursting at the seams just to get out of there. I wasn't made to stay in one place for too long —I got agitated. Avalon was a distant memory. Of course, I missed Marius and Lana, and Jazzy. But Oberon had sent me to Greece under false pretenses and he's been building an army to take Mount Olympus and hoping I will kill Zeus and become his weapon.

I'd been in Greece for almost a year and it was clear that people change over the course of their life depending on where that life takes them. Personally, I never imagined myself sitting in a castle having a philosophical discussion with a one-thousand-plus-year-old demon.

"Nathan, you've been around long enough to understand... we're not alone."

"True, I've been around a long time, but other than what I know or have seen myself, the possibility of multiple worlds never played a role in my existence—until recently."

"Then Oberon fucked it all up," I said quietly.

Nathan just looked at me, giving me time to digest everything. Realizing your entire existence was a lie made you question where you fit in.

"I know it's hard. Just realize that you're not on your own," Nathan said.

He stooped to kiss me. It was passionate, it was real. With my life going in so many different directions, Nathan was the only thing keeping me grounded. I never wanted to depend on anyone or rely on someone else for security. I was slipping but...I wanted that. Or did I? Gods forbid if something major came between us —I wouldn't be able to recover. I wasn't used to vulnerability.

"Ahem."

Raider loomed. Perfect moment ruined.

"What do you want?" Nathan said, agitated.

"You better come take a look."

Nathan stood up.

"You should come too," Raider said.

I arched an eyebrow and looked over at Nathan, then followed them toward the stairs. I heard the commotion before we reached the top of the staircase. The door to the gym flew off the hinges and crashed through to the wall in the foyer. We were about to walk in when a hanging bag came flying at us. What the fuck was it with the gym?

I put up a shield and the bag slammed into the barrier and exploded. What the fuck? There was no need to open the door to the weight room since it wasn't there anymore. The place was a complete disaster; the boxing ring had a huge hole in it and the ropes were singed or completely missing. Dem was lying in the corner with a massive hole in his chest. He was alive but looked incredibly pissed off. Zeus didn't look so happy either; he was lying against the other wall with half his jaw caved in. The room was silent.

"Does someone want to tell me what's going on here?" I asked.

"Why don't you ask him?" Dem motioned to Zeus.

The three of us turned to Zeus. His jaw had healed, and we stood waiting for an explanation.

"It doesn't matter," he grumbled.

With that, he got up and walked out. We looked at each other then turned to Dem. Tensions were high between everyone, the living situation was making us all a little claustrophobic.

"Either he leaves, or I do," Dem said and pushed himself off the floor and walked out.

Zeus would probably be at his temple, brooding. When I left the castle, I told Nathan I'd take care of it. Dem was more valuable to Nathan and Raider then Zeus would ever be.

The temple was empty, which was a given this time of day. I half expected Zeus to be sitting in a corner sulking, but he was standing by the wading pool looking in.

"You're not going to jump, are you?" I asked.

He turned to me and was silent, so I waited.

"If you are here to belittle me or to give me a big-fat fuck you, don't bother," he said.

"What's going on with you? The only reason you're there is because I vouched for you and promised you wouldn't cause any trouble."

"I never asked you to, and don't treat me like a child," he snapped.

"Then stop acting like one," I snapped back. "They're risking their lives for you to keep yours."

"They're using me," he said.

"So am I."

He was silent. I hated to admit it, but it was true.

"Look, you can't stay at the castle anymore," I said.

"I know," he said sadly.

"I have an idea. Nathan won't like it, but he'll have to deal."

I decided to stash Zeus at one of the townhouses behind the bar. Jen was more than willing; she said it made her feel safe knowing an all-powerful God was taking up residence behind the bar.

"*A*re you fucking nuts?!" Nathan yelled.

He was pissed. He jumped on me the moment I walked in and told him where I'd stashed Zeus. Nathan didn't care about him; he cared about possibly putting Jen at risk, now that the bar—and Jen's apartment—was almost back to normal.

"Where else did you want me to hide him, huh?" I said.

"I don't give a fuck. Where he *is* will put Jen in danger and I won't have that."

What was the extent of Nathan and Jen's relationship?

"What's your relationship with her?"

The look on his face told me he wasn't expecting that question.

"I don't know what you're talking about," he dodged.

"You're lying," I said.

"Raider and Jen have a relationship, everyone knows that," he dodged the question again.

"So did you." It wasn't a question.

The silence stretched between us. I had secretly wondered whether Nathan was carrying a torch for Jen, but the truth made me feel as though I was second best, like he was only with me because she was off the table.

"It was when we first came to Greece. She helped us settle in. It went on for a while till I realized it was Raider she secretly wanted."

"Did it bother you?" I asked.

"At first, but then I realized how happy they were, and I knew that we had been together out of convenience."

"Did you love her?" I asked.

"I thought I did."

"Why didn't you tell me?"

"I didn't want this type of reaction," he answered.

"Excuse me?"

"I didn't want you to get all jealous and blow it out of proportion."

I laughed. "I don't give a *fuck* about your past relationships. The fact that you didn't trust me enough to tell me pisses me off more than any relationship you had with her."

I walked out of his room and slammed the door to mine. I was running out of patience with our back and forth. Whenever we got together, something pulled us apart. Maybe it was because we were so much alike; maybe we were both crazy. *The thing is,* I thought, *nothing so drastic has come between us to really do much damage.* Later, I would look back and realize how wrong I was.

Zeus didn't care where he ended up. To smooth things over, I relocated him to the bed-and-breakfast I stayed at when I first came to Greece and got a room for myself, too. I was too pissed at Nathan to look at his face. My pride got in the way of my intelligence.

After my night in the hotel, Nathan called me to set up a meeting at the bar for later that morning. Obviously, he had spoken to Jen and she wanted to reassure me that I had nothing to fear. With Nathan so tight-lipped about everything, I was beginning to lose trust in him.

I stood outside the bar, staring at the large iron doors. It was the first time I saw the doors closed and a sense of foreboding and reluctance washed over me. It didn't feel like the welcoming place Jen had created. Jen. I had seen her every night keeping the soon-to-be-brides from making stupid decisions, keeping the band happy with top-shelf alcohol, and being the occasional therapist for the lost—lost like I had been when I first came to Plaka. I took a deep breath and imagined what Marius would say if he was here. *Don't be an idiot, Lex. You're the second-best assassin in Avalon. You face death every single fucking waking moment and you're scared of a few feelings? An awkward moment?*

With his voice in my head, I opened the massive doors and was hit with the strong smell of cleaner. Nathan was sitting on one of the high bar stools wrapping silverware into napkins and Raider was trying hard and failing at cutting limes into wedges—they were flat and would never fit into a beer bottle. I heard what sounded like Dem changing out keys downstairs, while Jen was behind the bar wiping the countertops and tap lines. Everyone turned toward me and I could only imagine what they saw. Me, silhouetted against the mid-morning sun. *This, Marius, these people and their judgment. This is what I am afraid of.*

I walked in and sat at the bar next to Nathan. After a bit, Dem joined us.

"Lex, I know you have questions about me. Maybe it's time I'm honest with you so you can understand that I'm not your enemy," Jen said.

I was quiet. Jen looked over at Nathan who was staring at me, waiting to see my reaction.

"I know about your connection to Marius. What is your connection to them?" I motioned to Nathan, Raider, and Dem.

Nathan offered up the answer.

"After what happened with Zeus, we decided to leave Olympus and come to Athens. To start over, I guess. However, your mind goes a little stir-crazy when you have nothing to focus on. We lost control and were bloodthirsty; thousands of years of war and death can change someone. We encountered Jen when we first came to Plaka."

I didn't ask whether they had been clients of Jen's. I was a little uncomfortable anyway.

"In my job, I don't ask what a person's past is, or what they're running from. When Nathan told me who they were, I trusted him enough to tell him the truth about me."

"What about you?" I asked. Besides being a madam for the Gods, what else was there? I was starting to get fidgety.

"I'm not human, not fully anyway," she answered.

"What are you then?" I asked impatiently.

"I'm a demigod; half God, half human," she explained.

I paused for a moment. "Stop, stop," I put my hands up. What the fuck had I gotten myself into with these people? Too late now. "Is there a pause button for this movie?" I asked.

"What?" Nathan said.

"Every time I turn around, something else is thrown at me. I have to start writing this shit down. I need a fucking road map— at least throw in an intermission between takes. What's next? You're gonna tell me Raider's really a woman?"

"What the fuck?" Raider growled.

Nathan and Dem laughed. They covered it up with a cough when Raider glanced over at them.

"I'm sorry, but I'm finding it really hard to keep up."

"Let me back up then," Jen explained. "Nathan and I getting together just happened."

"Honestly Jen, I don't care about your relationship with Nathan or Raider. I want to know why no one told me."

"I didn't want you not to trust me. When I saw you and Nathan getting closer, I thought if I told you it might ruin what you guys have," Jen said sincerely.

"I know you have a hard time trusting people, Lex. I want you to know, I'm not your enemy. Far from it."

I was quiet, trying to figure out how to respond. "Everyone in my life has fucked me over in some form or another," I said. Nathan stood up and walked out the door. He had trust issues; so did I.

"I understand, but it's very lonely out there all by yourself. You should know that," she responded.

There was no point in being angry anymore. Regardless of her reassurance, though, I was still gun-shy and needed time to adjust. To put it mildly, we were an interesting group; we didn't fully trust each other, but we didn't fully *not* trust each other either, if that made any sense.

I was hurt Nathan didn't tell me the truth. Didn't we at least trust each other? I guess we were keeping each other at arm's length, too scared to be fully honest with each other. This thing with Nathan was beginning to pull me in two different directions.

"What happened yesterday between you and Zeus?" I asked Dem.

"Ask him," he stated.

"I'm asking you," I said, frustrated.

"He wanted to give himself up to Oberon."

"What?" I asked, surprised.

"According to Zeus, he didn't seek you out to be turned into a bargaining chip. Also, if Nathan weren't so hell-bent on getting his revenge…"

"What are you talking about? What revenge?" I asked.

"Zeus and Nathan have a pretty bad history. You need to ask Nathan about that," Dem answered.

"Gods, this is giving me a headache," I said.

Afternoon would be here soon. I stood to leave, but Raider stopped me.

"What are you going to do?" he asked.

"Talk to Nathan. Apparently, no one has the balls to tell me the truth about anything," I answered.

I decided to flash to the castle. Dem and Raider were going to stay behind to help finish with the bar. Nathan and I were apparently on opposite pages when it came to our relationship. It was starting to get comfortable. Would we ever be in alignment? The door to his room loomed in front of me. I wasn't sure how this conversation would go, but we needed to get it over with if we were going to move on. I needed the whole truth from Nathan, instead of the pieces I was getting from everyone else. Obviously, they all had their secrets.

I raised my fist to knock, but the door opened first. Nathan looked less than happy to see me but I didn't really give a fuck. Someone needed to be the bigger person.

"Are you going to invite me in, or do you want to do this right here?" I said.

He moved out of the way and shut the door behind me. We were both silent for so long that I startled when he spoke.

"Sorry for being a dick," he said quietly.

"What? I couldn't hear you, could you say that again?"

"Don't be an asshole. My intentions were not to cause you harm in any way; I know I should have told you," he said.

"Yes, you should have. I want us to be able to trust each other, all of us. One minute we're on and then the next minute something comes between us, and that pattern is getting too comfortable. Nothing has come between us that we can't fix, but the fact that we keep finding ourselves here is getting a little old."

He walked over and caressed my face.

"I don't want that. I want us to be able to take on anything together. I trust you completely and I want you to trust me...to trust Dem and Raider as well. You're not alone. But I want you to promise me you won't leave, that you'll fight for us. I promise to do the same."

I smiled, pulled his face to mine and kissed him.

"I promise."

He returned the kiss, passionately, deeply. In that moment, I forgot about the stories I still needed to hear, the half-truths I was still untangling, and the lies that had made me furious minutes before. It was an obliterating kiss, but I'd come to regret letting the questions and the uncertainty go in that moment.

I suggested that Jen and I take some girl time and go shopping. Nathan was headed into Plaka as well and agreed to take us. It was a quiet drive. I sat in the passenger seat staring out the window. We were all on edge from the last couple days—well, the last year actually. Had I really been here that long? The days turned to months, the months to a year. Besides losing an entire month in a portal, I hadn't been doing much. Who knew my mission to locate and kill Zeus would be completely turned upside down by finding out who I was, and learning my mentor was the real enemy. Life had a real funny way of fucking you over.

Hades hadn't shown his face since Nathan ran into him. I was still in the dark about what had happened, and Nathan wouldn't elaborate. He dropped us off and said he was heading over to the bar to check on the guys. The streets were fairly busy for a weekday afternoon, but we window-shopped, pointing out things we liked.

"What's been going on between you and Raider?"

What can I say? I'm pretty blunt when I want to be. Jen looked my way and smiled.

"After Nathan and I ended our relationship, I all but declared a hiatus. I knew Raider had feelings for me, but it was awkward at first. He would come in the bar and flirt with every woman—available or not—who would look at him...and they all looked. He tried to smooth his way onto me, but I knew him too well for that."

Jen stopped and looked at a light-blue sundress on a mannequin—she seemed far away. "Anyway, one night the bar was busy and some of the patrons were getting a little rough. One guy attacked me because I wouldn't give him another drink

—Raider happened to come in at that moment and diffused the situation. He asked me out to dinner and we've been together ever since."

Raider was the supernatural version of a man slut, and every woman he hooked up with knew it, but didn't seem to mind. Jen was different. He truly cared for her; the signs were in the subtle way he looked at her and how he was around her. We walked into the boutique and Jen asked to try on the blue sundress, then she disappeared into the fitting room. I walked around the store, looking through the racks. Jen called me over to the dressing room. The dress looked amazing on her, she definitely had the look of a God.

"It looks great!" I smiled at her.

She grinned and walked back into the dressing room. Afterward, we walked out of the store and hailed a cab to this little Greek restaurant on the main strip that's hailed as the best in Plaka: Electra Palace Roof Garden. From there, the views of Athens are incredible. It always makes me smile to think that I'm part of this city, even though my life isn't the most relaxed or perfect, I wouldn't change this view for anything.

We ordered lunch. Jen asked for a glass of wine with her meal and I ordered a cocktail. I noticed Jen fidgeting with her napkin, looking anywhere but at me.

"Are you sure you want to go with us tonight?" I asked.

She was making me uneasy. She took a sip of wine and took a deep breath, trying to calm her nerves.

"I'm not going to lie, I'm a little nervous."

"So, why did you ask to come?"

She looked out toward Athens. Jen might be nervous, but I sensed she wasn't afraid.

"I've been here for many years. This place is my home and the guys are like family. If I don't do something to help, then I've failed them."

"Taking out Oberon? It isn't your fight, Jen," I told her.

She looked at me and smiled. "It's not yours either."

I laughed. "How do you figure?"

"You came here to find Zeus and take him out. Well, you found him...but decided to let him live because of what you found out about yourself. You stayed because you found yourself a part of something more than your own cause. You found people who care about you and who are willing to sacrifice everything for you."

"I don't know if Raider would agree with you."

She laughed at that. "Raider can be a bit rough around the edges, but like Nathan and Dem, there isn't anything he wouldn't do for the people around him. I think you fascinate him."

That statement made me feel a little awkward—Jen and Raider were a thing. She caught my nervousness and laughed wholeheartedly.

"What I mean is, you share a part of yourself that's similar. A part that you might not always be able to control, but you know there are people around you who will always keep you grounded."

After lunch, we paid the tab and caught a cab back to the bar. The short drive gave me a little time to ponder what Jen had said. I'd always noticed something different about her, something not altogether normal. The sun was starting to set, and I was getting anxious. The bar was coming together and I was excited for Jen to reopen it. Over the last year, it had become a staple in my life; a place where I had family. I stared at the bar, lost in thought and Nathan took my hand and I smiled.

"What are you looking at?" he asked.

"Just reminiscing. Thinking about how much everything is going to change or has changed."

Nathan turned me to look at him. "Hey, whatever happens tonight, it will all work out."

"I know. I'm just a little on edge, I guess," I said.

He smiled at me. "Everything's going to be fine. Don't worry."

I touched his face and smiled. "I know."

He leaned in and kissed me. Slowly at first, then deeper, like he may never get the chance again. When he pulled away and I looked in his eyes, I saw sadness. A dull pain hit me in the heart. That was weird. I reached up and caressed his face.

"Hey, you okay?"

He took my hand, turning it over palm up, then he kissed it and gave me a small smile.

"Just tired."

I kissed him one more time, giving him reassurance. Before long, I'd come to realize that what was happening tonight wouldn't matter much—not in the end anyway.

The night came too fast; it was like the dark was anticipating what was about to happen and wanted to get it over with. I was also afraid for Jen. Sure, she was immortal, but she was still putting herself at risk. Raider was taking it pretty well, all things considered. Jen was just as capable as the rest of us and it made sense that she wanted to be involved, after all her girls had been used and slaughtered.

We hopped in the SUV and drove to the club together; Zeus chose to stay behind for some reason. I wondered if Ares would make an appearance, he hadn't been seen since the portal opened in the weight room. Was he waiting in a dark corner for us to drop our defenses? Okay, so that's a little melodramatic, but come on, it is Ares after all. I stared out the window, watching the world pass by. Something kept eating at me; it was a feeling that something was about to change everything, that something was going to change me.

Unfortunately, the club was packed, but we had no control over that. Jen headed for the bar and Raider watched her the whole way. He was worried. Nathan and Dem split up, heading in different directions and blending in with the crowd. I was to keep an eye on Jen, with Raider refusing to leave my side.

Something was off. I looked around, trying to pinpoint what

was putting me on edge. Those familiar eyes landed on me and I almost lost my breath, but instead, I lost my footing and nearly face-planted in front of a room full of people. Thankfully, Raider steadied me.

"Shit," I said.

Raider looked around, trying to figure out what I was looking at. "What is it?"

"We need to leave. Now!" I said it without looking at him.

"What? Why?"

I looked over at the bar and saw Jen ordering a drink. She wasn't alone, though. A few guys had circled around her, trying their best to woo her away, but Jen was having none of it. Those eyes kept staring at me; I'd recognize that stare anywhere: Lucian. A man I had once considered a mentor and a friend.

All of that had changed when he revealed the true depths of his cruelty. I watched him enjoy torturing people. He would bring them close to death, revive them, and start again. He used to say he was giving us an educational lesson, but it made me sick. He made Hades look like a big teddy bear.

Raider stepped in front of me to get my attention and shook my shoulders to jolt me from my far-off stare.

"Lex, what's wrong with you?"

I snapped out of it and looked up at him. "Get Jen out of here."

Raider looked over at the bar. Jen was sitting by herself, staring at us—she shrugged her shoulders. I looked back and saw Lucian making his way toward her. I took off through the crowd, pushing people out of my way. What would happen if Lucian reached her before I did? Most people were so drunk they didn't even notice me, but one guy grabbed me and pulled me to the dance floor. Without hesitation, I pushed him off, throwing him into the crowd.

I lost Lucian for a moment and part of me was relieved—maybe I'd imagined the whole thing. That reprieve didn't last very long. With no time to react, Lucian appeared in front of my unsuspecting face, followed immediately by Raider. That was a surprise; I didn't even know he'd been following me. Lucian sized Raider up.

"Really?" Lucian chuckled.

I nonchalantly looked around to make sure the others were nearby.

"What are you doing here?" I snapped.

Lucian smiled. "Now, is that any way to greet an old friend?"

Out of my peripheral vision I glimpsed Raider clenching his jaw. He'd lose it pretty soon, and a pissed-off Raider is not something I wanted to see again.

"I'm checking up on your progress. I know you've been in contact with Marius, and he tells me you've got everything under control. However, I think he's lying."

"I know the truth, Lucian. I'm not playing by Oberon's rules anymore."

Lucian raised an eyebrow and studied me. I tried to push Raider away from me without Lucian noticing, but Raider was stubborn as shit. He didn't even budge.

"Guess that ruins the surprise. What are you going to do, Lex? Take out an entire army by yourself? Your friends won't help you. They have just as much to lose as you. One thing you forget: I know you better than you think I do, so watch your back," Lucian seethed.

Lucian threw Raider across the room, overturning a few booths. It didn't faze anyone, they just danced around us. Humans surprised me: if World War III were raging behind them, they'd just think a mosh pit was getting out of hand. Lucian advanced; he didn't even need to touch me.

"You won't win, Lex. You keep playing the way you are and you will get burned," he hissed.

I saw Raider get up and stalk toward us. Nathan and—I'll be royally fucked—Hades headed our way, too. Guess the search for Hades was off, or it was another lie.

"Is that a threat?" I growled.

"Facts, Lex. Just facts."

He looked over at the guys, then back at me.

"Remember what I said."

He flashed out and I was left there dumbfounded about what was unfolding. Nathan, Raider, and Hades were all heading my way—together. I didn't care who saw me. I flashed in front of Hades, withdrew the knife from my boot and had every intention of cutting off his fucking head until Nathan held me back. I struggled to get him off, but his grip just got tighter.

"Stop!" Nathan said.

I looked up at him, confusion all over my face. "What the hell are you doing? Let me go," I growled.

"No." His voice was flat as concrete.

I blinked. "What did you just say to me?" I asked, dumbfounded.

"Lex," he began.

I flashed back to the house, leaving him alone with whatever he wanted to say next. I paced my room, picking up anything in my reach and throwing it against the wall. It didn't help; it just pissed me off even more. I'd been fuming for a while when Nathan came into the room and ducked as I threw a lamp at his head.

"What did you say to me about Zeus, huh? You said I couldn't touch him."

I rounded on him. "That's not the same."

"Really? How do you figure?"

"He didn't nearly cut off your head and leave you for dead behind a fucking bar!" I yelled.

"He ruined my life!" Nathan bellowed. He took a deep breath and calmed down. "This isn't about you, Lex. Hades and I made a deal."

I laughed. "The same deal you made with Zeus?"

Nathan was quiet.

"Must be a pretty sweet deal to have you turn into their bitch."

"I'm not going to fight with you," he said.

Usually Nathan's voice calmed me, but right now I wanted to rip his fucking head off. I tried to leave, but Nathan got in my way.

"Move," I growled.

"No."

"Get out of my fucking way, Nathan."

"You're not leaving until you talk to me. You promised me you wouldn't do this."

"That was before you chose Hades over me."

Nathan tried to grab me, to stop me from leaving, but I turned and punched him. He flew across the room, hitting the wall with so much force it crumbled underneath him. I walked out of the room and grabbed my leather jacket from the coat rack. He jumped up and followed me downstairs. I was headed toward the front door when Hades just had to open his fucking mouth.

"Lovers' quarrel?" he chuckled.

That did it. I flashed in front of him, took out my knife, and shoved it in his eye, pushing that thing all the way to the back of his fucking skull. He screamed and fell to his knees. Blood sprayed everywhere. Some got on me, but I didn't even care. Dem, Raider, Zeus, and Jen came out of the entertainment room and stopped. How the hell did they get here so fast? They all stared at Hades as he tried to wrench the knife from his eye.

"Very mature," Nathan said from behind me.

I ignored him and headed for the front door, but Nathan snagged my arm.

"Lex, please."

I looked at his hand then up into his eyes and yanked my arm out of his grasp.

"Don't fucking touch me," I snarled.

I put on my jacket and walked out. My head was screaming. I

walked past Nathan's Mustang and with just a thought, it exploded. The flames warmed my body, igniting something inside of me: anger, hatred. Someone called my name, but I didn't care. I climbed in the Maserati and peeled out of the driveway. I felt sick, like I had to get out of there. I watched the castle and Plaka disappear in the rear-view mirror. For once in my life I had nothing, like everything around me had vanished and I was alone for the first time.

It's hard to explain what was going on in my head, but it was the only thing that kept me going. That cold place was screaming at me to run. To say "fuck you" to everyone, to leave and not come back. But when I thought about what lay ahead of us, I grew roots. As much as I wanted to, shit was about to hit the fan and I needed to be there. I couldn't leave.

I drove to the beach, parked, and walked to the water's edge. It was peaceful, like the oasis I'd visited in the portal a few months ago. I sat and looked out at the ocean. I was so angry at Nathan, so hurt. I understood what he'd said about Zeus—that Zeus had ruined his life, but he'd been willing to ally with him in spite of it —but I was having a hard time accepting his decision about Hades. What would happen next? What did this mean for me? Everything was about to change. My trust for Nathan had just been thrown out the window. I was broken. My life, my love. I was being tested, made to ask how hard I was willing to hold on, and I sensed everything slipping through my fingers. I stood at the edge of this life and jumped.

END OF BOOK ONE

ACKNOWLEDGMENTS

I want to thank Lauren Taylor Shute, who was there since the beginning. She held my hand through the whole process and heard my tears and excitement. She took a chance on me and I will forever be grateful.

Special thanks to everyone on the Lauren Taylor Shute Editorial team who helped make this book possible, including Shannon Henesy, whose editorial assistant work kept us all on our toes, Chantai Thomas for her help in the project's early stages, Allyson Rudolph for her keen editorial work, and Evie Carrick for her copyediting skills.

I also want to thank the wonderful Hampton Lamoureux for my cover design. You have brought to life my imagination, and it is beautiful.

ABOUT THE AUTHOR

Photo by Shannon Brown

Katharine Ann Melton was raised in Northern California, where she read and admired Greek and Roman mythology from an early age. She now lives in the Washington D.C. metro area. *Behind the Mirage* is her first novel.

Connect with the author at **www.KatharineAnnMelton.com** to receive updates on the next book in the series, exclusive content, and more.

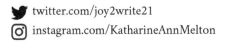

twitter.com/joy2write21
instagram.com/KatharineAnnMelton